SAVAGE HEARTS

BOOK ONE IN THE SAVAGE HEARTS SERIES

MARY E. TWOMEY

For every woman who stood by me
during this ridiculously hard year.

I see you, and I am grateful you saw me.

ACT OR ACCEPT

ADELITA

"You were supposed to be gone by seven," Tomás scolds me on speakerphone as I straighten up my office. I can picture his rounded chin turning from left to right while he wears his usual good-natured grin. He always lectures me with a smile.

Warmth spreads through my arms when it's clear that he cares. It's a comfort to know that anyone cares if I'm the last therapist here. I sometimes stay too late tidying up the building, but honestly, how is my patient with crippling OCD supposed to have a productive session if the office isn't presentable?

"My last patient needed the extra ten minutes. I'm just packing up for the night, I promise. Lara is coming your way now." Then in a singsong voice, I add, "Put on your gracious smile for her mother."

I don't have the courage to tell Tomás that I wouldn't dare stay much later tonight.

For three days now, I've had the distinct feeling that I'm being followed. I've been careful, not doing anything extraordinary that might make me stand out, but still I feel the eyes every time I walk out of the office or my apartment.

Mama warned me about this. We moved around so much because she was afraid my birth father was following us. It's been two years since she passed. I assumed the stalking would have ended then. It was her he was after, not me.

Never me.

Tomás sighs heavily before he ends the call, and I chuckle because I completely understand. Lara, my last patient on Tuesdays, doesn't travel with her own personal sunshine. That is most likely because Lara's mother is the storm that shows up with no warning or reason, demanding to be obeyed at any volume she good and well pleases.

Fun times. I only have to deal with the antagonistic mother one hour a week. I cannot imagine Lara's stress.

I tap my scheduler app, making sure I'm up to date on all my patients' needs. The orange pillows on my leather couch flourish nicely with a few fluffs, looking just about perfect when I set them back down. One of my patients tomorrow is a twelve-year-old on the spectrum who suffers from many things, not the least of which is an anxiety disorder. I don't want anything to set her off. The fuzzy side of the pillows are turned around so she doesn't have to see or touch them.

The evening comes sooner and sooner as the weeks have grown colder. I hope my lavender cardigan will be enough to fend off the early autumn chill.

I smile conspiratorially at Tomás on the way out. He's trying not to argue with Lara's mother. The poor, miserable woman insists on always being right, even though she rarely is.

Tomás' eyes widen for a moment with sheer exasperation, but then flick back to the appointment book to figure out where Lara could best fit. "I'm sure we can find something to work with Lara's theater schedule. The twentieth won't do?"

Lara opens her mouth, but her mother speaks for her—a thing I've been coaching them both through. "The twentieth is the dress rehearsal for Lara's show. The big show. The one I've mentioned at least four times in the past two weeks. I can tell you listen about as well as her shrink."

She leans her elbow on Tomás' desk. I know she sees I'm standing right here, but she doesn't bother to coat her words with anything resembling sugar or politeness.

"Honestly, her eyes are freakish. I can barely listen to her half the time because I'm trying to figure out how she got that horrific genetic defect."

Sure. My eyes are the reason she can't listen.

I purse my lips. My eyes are blue, which sure, is an anomaly, but it's not like I can help that I stand out from the sea of varying shades of brown eyes that exist in nearly every other person in the world.

Apparently, that's a trait I got from my birth father. I know approximately two things about him: he stalked my mother and he has eyes the color of sapphires, like me.

I've long since passed the point where I feel the need to justify my appearance or myself to people, but that one detail has been the constant slow drip from birth.

I dip my hand into my pocket and squeeze my stress toy. Most of my patients use a squishy ball and grip it when they feel agitated. My stress object is a tungsten tube half the length of a pencil. It's supposed to be the strongest steel in the world. I watched videos of the world's self-proclaimed toughest man trying to bend a tungsten rod, and he couldn't.

Of course, the little rods hadn't been tested on the world's strongest woman.

I have a whole box of these tungsten tubes that I've bent or broken while trying to hide my stress.

Come on, Lara. We went over this. Act or accept. Act or accept.

You can act by speaking up for yourself, or you can accept your mother's acerbic behavior, which makes you complicit.

Lara says nothing the entire time her mother degrades me and Tomás, which is no real surprise. It's an indicator that she still hasn't found her voice.

That's what therapy is for. We'll get there.

I examine the scene closer, trying to really see the teenager who is always trying to disappear in plain view. Judging by the way Lara looks forlornly at her shoes and then with a pleading look at Tomás to please forgive her mother's acerbic demeanor, I can tell that yes, perhaps Lara has found her voice. She just doesn't know what to do with it. She doesn't trust it enough to put volume to her heart.

Perhaps Lara's convinced that if she dares voice who she is, it won't matter to the universe. That *she* won't matter.

I can understand that.

I love my job. It allows me to connect with people while still keeping them at a distance. Connect and release, connect and release.

It's a good rhythm for me. I don't like things too intense.

Tomás catches my eye and releases a deep breath that moves his bulbous belly. It reminds us both to exhale through the insults, the insinuations, and the general crap that comes when you've signed on to help humanity long after they've run out of answers.

I give him a bolstering smile with my eyes crossed just to give him a little comic relief. I'm grateful for my office ally.

I move through the exit and inhale the gorgeous perfume of the outdoors. Sure, it's got notes of asphalt, cinnamon from the churro shop next door and about a thousand cigarette butts that litter the walkway, but I can also pick out the fragrance of foliage. Pops of nature line the quaint parking lot, along with the few flowers that have held on to the very end of the season and dared set foot into the next.

There's another bit of poetry I'm grateful for. Some days I'm so surrounded by melancholy and angst that I cling to the pops of beauty, however sparse. The flowers are a bright spot in my evenings, so I make a point not to take them for granted.

My feet stop short on the way to my silver sedan. I look behind me, flipping my shoulder-length wavy black hair to check to see if Lara followed behind. I feel eyes on me again, but when I turn, she's not there. She's still in the building, no doubt silently dying inside while her mother talks down to Tomás.

I know well the difference between paranoia and a true worry. The feeling of being watched is no dismissible notion. My keys are clutched in my fist as I keep walking.

This time when I stop again, it's because Lara and her mother are clicking their heels to their car. The red mustang is a source of contention between the two of them. It belonged to Lara's grandmother, and she doesn't feel right being in it, now that her grandmother has passed.

Lara's mother took over ownership of it the second her own mother was diagnosed with cancer, along with many other trinkets from the home. It was like watching a legal theft take place.

That had been a series of long therapy sessions in which I tried not to internalize and compare their situation to my own.

My mama had done her best, with both of us working two jobs apiece to put me through college. We took the bus and ate beans so I could get an education. Once I graduated and got my first career job, the plan was for me to buy us a car just like the used silver sedan I'm walking towards now, so Mama never had to take the bus again.

I scrunch my eyes shut to scrub my mind of the bus crash that left me an orphan on the way home from my college graduation. I'd been wearing my cap and gown still, because Mama insisted I never take it off. She bragged to everyone on the bus that day that her daughter was a college graduate.

I bite my lip through the flash of golden eyes, long black hair and skin a shade of brown darker than mine who pulled me from the crash. Me, but not Mama. Me, and no one else.

His face still haunts my dreams.

Santiago.

He's the only other person with oddly-colored eyes I've ever seen.

When he dragged me out of the wreckage, all I could comprehend was his name and a string of syllables that he spoke over my body with the reverence of one casting forth a blessing. When he finished, there was a note of contentment, like he was proud of a job well done. "Now you'll only be as strong as you are gentle."

I didn't get out a full sentence before he kissed my forehead, laid my shaking form on the concrete and ran.

I see his face in my mind at least once a day, though it's been two years since that horrible afternoon.

I didn't need *more* power. I was already born with too much. I'd needed my mama, but what he gave me was an increase in the ability to do things like bend steel as easily as one bends a plastic straw.

Lucky me.

I swallow hard, reminding myself that it's been two years since the crash. I should be able to get through an entire day without feeling the jarring terror of the bus crash. I should be able to walk to my car without visualizing the man with golden eyes. I shouldn't hear Santiago's voice, filled with wonder over the grand gift of too much strength he was unleashing in me. It had been a struggle to hide my strength growing up. Now I have to be extra careful because my muscle is tied to how gentle I am.

I should be able to look at my car without missing my mama.

I roll back my shoulders and push out the melancholy with a few measured breaths. I unlock my door and reach for the handle, but the thing refuses to open. I frown, confused that anything gives me pause. I've never had a door stick in my life.

My brow furrows as I stare at the handle, completely flummoxed.

I grip once more and tug, but only manage to rip the silver handle clear off the door.

¡Carajo!

Quickly, I bury my fist in my pocket, horrified that I've slipped up out in the open.

Lara tucks herself in her mother's car. Her mother slams her own door shut without noticing my misstep, texting up a storm as she starts driving. It's the one time I'm grateful Lara's mother doesn't notice the world around her, though I worry for everyone else on the road she travels.

I grimace at the sight of the torn-off handle in my fist as I take it back out of my cardigan pocket. Not for the first time, I'm confused at my own ridiculous strength.

Though no one's there to witness my befuddlement, I feel someone watching. Careful to check the parking lot for anyone nearby, I work my fingers into the groove between the door and the car, and do what I can to pry the thing open. It's not cold enough for ice to have set in and fused the door shut. Though even this option has me shaking my head. I'm stronger than ice.

Tomás trots out of the building and waves at me. "Have a good night, Adelita."

"You too, Tomás." I try to sound and appear casual as I meander to my passenger's side door and pop that open with no issue. I scoot in, feeling foolish as I crawl over the console so I can get into my own driver's seat.

I don't even work my keys into the ignition before I realize the source of that eerie "being watched" feeling.

I didn't notice the two men in cut-offs and camo t-shirts before, but now I see them running for Tomás. The sweet receptionist's only defense is a bleat of fear before he's shoved roughly to the ground. His round chin skips on the asphalt and the contents of his messenger bag spills all over the ground.

"Hey!" I shout, but the two attackers don't turn towards me.

Act or accept. Act or accept.

It's unclear if the muscular men are armed, if they're trying to rob Tomás, or what exactly they want. But as they've pushed the meek secretary, I decide I have all the information I need to involve myself.

Tomás makes my life easier by respecting my schedule and not making appointments for me outside my set days. We knit coffee cup cozies on our lunch breaks together for every new patient. Who would hurt a precious soul like that?

My door is still stuck but I don't have it in me to waste time crawling back out the passenger's side to confront them. Tomás is crying and guarding his face in a ball on the ground.

No part of me can accept this.

I have to get out there.

Something in me snaps. Without bothering with the handle, I shove at the driver's side door with my shoulder, confused at the metallic screech when it bangs open.

I don't worry about the weirdness of my car, but push everything out of my mind as I glower at the men who have got nothing better to do than beat up on poor Tomás.

"Let him go!" I should really start carrying pepper spray. If they don't back off him, I might have to resort to force.

I'm not worried about losing in a fist fight; I dread winning. I don't want to think about how bloody it all might get if they don't back down.

I stop halfway there, hoping desperately that they scatter.

One of the two assailants—a guy with a narrow face and slicked-back black hair pulled into a man bun juts his chin out at me, almost like he's actually about to negotiate. His eyes alight on mine as if he knows me.

As if he was waiting for *me*, not Tomás.

He spreads his arm out, presenting the prize that is Tomás. "If you want him, come and get him."

There's a calmness to his challenge. This is what he was hoping would happen.

No one knows I'm strong. He couldn't possibly. I've never seen Man Bun before in my life.

Tomás whimpers, so I decide it's worth the risk of my secret getting exposed to make sure Tomás gets home safely to his plump cat. Caesár isn't going to feed himself tonight.

The second aggressor has ratty braids that whip around his head when he turns his chin to Man Bun. "You need more proof than her busting out of the car? We sealed that thing. There's no way she's not one of his." He motions to my face, as if that's another thing to prove his point.

My eyebrows raise at the notion that I might belong to anyone.

Man Bun sizes up my car, not like he's going to steal it, but like he's impressed I could open the door with which they'd evidently tampered.

I want to book them both for an appointment so we can deal with their violent proclivities. Instead, my focus drifts to my poor friend. "Tomás, is anything broken?"

"No," he works out in a choked sob.

I hate seeing Tomás cry. Once he had tears in his eyes when his other cat, Misker Whiskers, passed on. I couldn't stop bringing Tomás tea and offering him tissues. I deal with drawing out emotions in people all day long, but the sweet ones who cry over animals and precious things like that always get me in my soft spots.

Tomás' eyes catch on mine from across the parking lot. "Run, Adelita! Save yourself."

Everything in me softens. "Oh, *chiquito*, I'm not leaving you. Close your eyes." It probably sounds like I'm trying to be kind and save him from seeing violent things, but that's only part of it. Truly, I'm saving him from learning my secret. I'm saving myself from explaining my abnormalities that I haven't been able to reason through myself.

"We have to be sure," says Long Braids. "Father won't tolerate us bringing in the wrong girl again."

I frown when it sounds like they're talking about me being the reason they're here, even though it seemed like Tomás was their mark.

Who is their dad, and what could he possibly want with me?

The men in camo stalk towards me but I wait until Tomás' lashes sweep shut before I run at Man Bun.

I'm not a trained fighter, but I don't need to be. It's almost no effort at all to cuff Man Bun around the throat. I'm angry that anyone might hurt someone who knits coffee cup cozies, as if the world has buckets and buckets of people like that.

My hands are shaking, my rage clashing with fear of my strength that might never go away, and bringing both to the surface. I am not a violent person. I don't want any part of this. But given the choice between *accepting* that Tomás would be beaten up or *acting* on an impulse to save him, I decide to deal with the guilt of participating in a brawl later.

Man Bun's pulse jumps under my touch, as if he's offering up his heartbeat for me to hold. Maybe he thinks I'll be merciful, but the terror in his eyes tells me he's starting to rethink his life's choices.

People don't fear me. They mostly ignore me. The few who do know me smile in my direction when I round the corner. But this stranger whose name I don't even know stares into my freakishly blue eyes, his brown ones bulging.

I'm guessing it's just now dawning on him that whatever he thought he was getting into by messing with Tomás, he had no idea.

Man Bun tries to claw at my arm so he can choke in a breath, but my grip only tightens around his throat.

Though I'm not fluid with my motions, it's easy to squeeze too hard as I shove him backward into Tomás' car. I don't mean to dent the hood with Man Bun's body, but a choked puff of agony emanates into the air.

Terror slices through me. I know I've gone too far.

That little fact turns my insides into pure chaos. I don't kill people. I recycle. I hug my patients.

I stare at my hand as if I don't understand what it's doing. "You hurt him!" I explain to my victim as I panic, my conscience warring at the prospect of repaying violence with violence.

Is this who I am? Would Mama be proud of me for unleashing like this?

Though the criminal is struggling beneath my grip, it's Santiago's bright golden eyes I see in my imagination.

"Strength should be measured with gentleness. Use both wisely. Now you'll only be as strong as you are gentle."

Fresh from a bus crash, I hadn't grasped the gravity of those words when Santiago first pulled me out.

I loosen my grip on Man Bun's throat and instead coil my fingers around his wrist, snapping several important bones.

Wrist bones are far easier to break than tungsten tubes, and they make noises infinitely more satisfying.

I don't like this side of me.

"Are you still torn? It's obviously her!" Long Braids shouts, his hands gripping my shoulders from behind to jerk me off his friend.

It's a bad move on his part. My elbow aims for his gut, but I miss horribly and crack a couple of Long Braids' ribs. The quick movement costs me barely any effort, but my conscience screams.

Panic pours out of me. "Oops! I'm sorry! I didn't mean to do that!"

This is why I shouldn't fight.

Long Braids doubles over, holding his side as he howls. His nonsensical swearing hits the air in time with his knees smacking the pavement.

I slap Man Bun's head against the hood of the car once more, harder than I mean to. I hope I haven't cracked his skull, only knocked him out.

His body sags and slips to the concrete, giving me the space to breathe, and my conscience the room to bleed out in the open.

I didn't mean for this to happen.

2

SLEEP BABY SLEEP
ADELITA

I touch my forehead, but I'm only just beginning to sweat from the worry of being exposed for the freak I am. Two years of keeping things quiet are gone now as Long Braids howls through his pain, bending over to cradle his cracked ribs.

But since Tomás is still breathing, I wager it all as the right choice.

Except that Man Bun isn't moving from his place on the pavement where his limp body slid. Bile churns in my stomach. I force myself to look away, focusing on the scared look in Tomás' eyes.

I kneel down and brush a curl from Tomás' forehead. "Are you okay, *Chiquito*? Should I call you an ambulance?"

His lower lip trembles. Despite my firm command that he keep his eyes closed, it's clear he's seen too much. "How d-d-did you do that? I saw you break his... And then you... Adelita?"

My lips purse to keep the expletive inside. "You definitely hit your head. I'll call the paramedics."

I have no training in things like this. I studied hard, my

nose in a book until it was time to clean houses with Mama after school. No one told me not to take your eye off your target.

When I reach for my phone in my pocket, I don't see Long Braids come at me until it's too late.

I'm strong, but not necessarily strategic.

Getting stabbed is something you see in movies and hear about in vague circumstances that have nothing to do with you. When the blade sinks into my shoulder from behind, I'm positive my brain must be mistaken.

A sharp laugh cracks into the air and all coherent thought leaves me. In the bustling world, there is only this moment, only this shock that after everything, my life will end so very stupidly with my mama nowhere in sight.

I don't feel the pain at first, only waves of disbelief that something so horrifying is happening to me.

Adelita Corazón, the first female valedictorian in the history of Acosta Elementary.

Adelita Corazón, only child of Camila Corazón, who was a cleaning lady and selfless saint.

Adelita Corazón, Licensed Therapist and prairie novel enthusiast.

Adelita Corazón, whose blood is staining her shirt as her dark hair whips around her face.

I have my mama's features—a heart-shaped face, a nose that's somehow both wide-ish and buttoned, and full lips that never opened to cut anybody's confidence.

And now I'm dying, but in my mind's eye, it's her whom I picture bleeding. It's Mama's sweet yet determined demeanor draining out onto the pavement for anyone to carelessly trample over.

A gust of cold wind hits from out of nowhere. It's not just a breeze, but a powerful slap across the face from Mother Nature. It's the only thing I feel—so great is my shock over the blade in my shoulder. If I was standing, no doubt the blast would have blown me backwards.

At the sight of the crimson on my pink blouse, lavender cardigan and gray slacks, my brain catches up and the pain hits me like a freight train. I work out a strangled scream but it's overshadowed by the crack of a cry from Long Braids, who stumbles backward.

He stabbed *me*. Not sure why his scream is louder than mine. I crawl over to Tomás and slump over his body, shielding him as best I can while I shudder through the agony.

The harsh wind whips my hair and tugs at my cardigan. I'm certain the pain of each breath will end my life. My mind struggles to process a blade in my shoulder.

I blink and realize there are new people in the parking lot now, but I don't know when they got here. Two men in jeans and matching black t-shirts stand over us. They emanate assurance and bravery, as if this scene is already under control, even though I don't see how it possibly could be.

I hold Tomás, sheltering him from the wind as best I can. I hope the newcomers are here to help.

My heart stutters when I hear a growl from an enormous wolf. The animal is easily the size of my desk.

I hear myself scream. I know my heart is doing its best not to give out from the mix of shock and pain.

The two newcomers in black t-shirts are equally incensed and graceful as they smash Long Braids against the side of Tomás' car. One of them holds Long Braids' arms out so their victim is vulnerable. "Do it, Cruz!"

The larger one with broad shoulders, who I'm guessing is Cruz, is composed as he rams a knife into Long Braids' stomach. Blood spills a few inches below the ribs I cracked.

Good guys, I tell myself through pained breaths. *They're the good guys. I won't have to fight them, too.*

Cruz's eyes are impassive as he slices a line across the man's abdomen, fileting my attacker open. "Why are you here?" Cruz thunders. "This is farther from the caves than your people usually travel." As he interrogates the man, the clouds overhead turn dark with malice, which matches his mood.

Cruz's voice sends chills through me with the power his cadence commands. I feel small, huddled on the pavement a few feet from his massive form while Tomás whimpers beneath me.

Long Braids finds the gumption to answer, even through his injuries. "She belongs to us. I'm not leaving without having collected her!" He gasps through his pain. "And if I fail, then the others will not stop until we have her!"

Ice races through my body. Who are these people, and what could they possibly want with me?

I don't know who Cruz is, but I could not fathom disobeying him, fierce as he looks with his stern, wide jaw and short black hair that doesn't dare move with the wind. He's tall and muscular, thick around the chest, and clearly in charge, since the wolf and the other man in a black t-shirt are looking to him to determine their next move.

The wolf seems more sentient than your average canine, zeroed in on Cruz rather than letting his maw whip around with scattered focus.

When Cruz twists the blade in Long Braids' stomach, there is no remorse or thrill in his eyes. He's emotionless and determined, going along with his evening's plan, as if murder is a mere item on his checklist.

The wind chills me, but the deadened look in Cruz's brown eyes ices me over.

Good guy, I remind myself, only this time less certain. *He's the good guy.*

The wolf sniffs my shoulder. Though I've gone

completely still, a high-pitched bleat of terror escapes my lips at the massive maw so very near. Then, as if sensing I can't take the suspense a second longer, the black-furred creature sits beside me and angles his jaw over Tomás. His eyes are golden, and lock in on mine in an almost human way. It's a protective stance he's taking, guarding Tomás beside me so I'm not alone in this.

If I was brave, I would hug this giant wolf. But logic takes over, so I remain frozen in my fear.

Long Braids chokes out a reply that's so acerbic; I'm not sure he realizes he's inches away from death. Now should be a time for pleading, not bravado. Still, he jerks his chin to the man who is not Cruz, who is holding him in place. "My imbunche pet would never be let off his leash, as you are. Unworthy cows, all of you!" Then Long Braids has the gall to spit in the man's face. He barks out a cruel laugh. He's got to be half-insane with how close he is to his last breath.

Wasting your final seconds on mockery is a life choice I will never understand.

Every breath is a slice through my entire being, rattling each nerve. No matter how captivating the intensity of the scene unfolding before me has become, I'm unable to distract myself from the agony in my shoulder.

"Tomás," I whisper as the wind belts across my body. I'm begging him to help me, to make the pain stop.

I need him to somehow get us out of here.

I want to hear my mama's voice so badly; I'm afraid my heart might die of neglect if I don't.

But Tomás doesn't answer. I'm not sure he can.

When I finally wrestle my phone from my pocket, it's a hefty debate of if I should call the paramedics or if I should dial my voicemail to play the recording of her asking me to pick up milk on my way home from work. She sang it to me. Who does something so cute and silly over a grocery item?

The pain in my shoulder is so acute, I can't think straight. I want only her. If she was here, surely this wouldn't be happening.

My debate stalls the second my arm goes numb and the phone slips from my hand. Poor Tomás has fainted on the concrete beneath me.

The wolf still guarding us is unable to call the paramedics or replay my mama's song to soothe me.

My body shivers against the harsh whip of the wind. The small shudder seems to be the last bit of energy I have in my arsenal. My vision narrows as my body bleeds.

I can't reach my phone to hear Mama's voice. I need her so badly.

To compensate for the loss, my imagination plays back the song Mama used to sing to me every night when I was a little girl, and then a teenager (too big for such things), and even as an adult.

"Sleep, baby, sleep.
Dream, baby, dream.
Love, baby, love.
My baby, mine."

THE NUMBNESS in my arm spreads into my chest, slowing my heart rate to a thrum too quiet for even Mama's lullaby.

The wolf at my side leans toward me and rests his throat over my arm, whining about my pain, like it hurts him to see me like this. Then he angles his maw up and fixes me with golden eyes so understanding, I want to weep on his furry shoulder and confess all my sins.

I didn't study hard enough for my Master's thesis.

I didn't feed the stray cats in our neighborhood as often as I should've.

I don't know my new neighbor's name because I've been too busy being antisocial.

I saw a piece of trash on the sidewalk yesterday and didn't pick it up.

His black fur contrasts with his bright golden eyes, warming me with understanding, even though I can't work out how to open my mouth. He has a scarred face with whole chunks of fur missing, like someone's burned this poor puppy's left cheek and temple.

My brain splutters in too many directions. I want to beg him to help me, beg him to call the ambulance, beg him to let me hear my mama's voice, but none of that comes to my lips.

Meek. That's what his eyes convey. While the big man doing the stabbing was aggressive and in charge, the representative from the animal kingdom is gentle. If only there was more meekness in the world.

I decide not to resist when he sniffs my uninjured shoulder.

He wraps his tail around my waist and steps a paw over my body, shielding me from the harsh wind as much as he's able. His eyes are telling me to trust him, but I can't imagine how something like trust matters in this moment, which is surely my last.

Cruz, the big man in charge, lets out a grunt as he slits Long Braids' throat. Cruz ignores my raspy scream as my attacker crumples in a pile of limbs on the concrete. Then he bends down and wipes his knife off on the dead man's shorts.

Cruz turns to the wolf, who's still trying to soothe me with his gentle gaze. "Santos, do what you can to bandage her up. You heard that guy. More are coming. They didn't show up to abduct just any random woman; they came specifically for her, and they're not going to stop until they have her.

We've got to get her out of here before more of them show up."

My mind drifts into an abyss of pain so great, I cannot comprehend it. I can't make sense of the trees that are whipping under the violent urges of the sudden wind. I can't make out the sharp words of the stern-jawed Cruz any longer, even as he gives orders to his other friend on two legs.

My vision tunnels until the world goes dark.

Mama's voice finds me, cradling my soul in that way she always managed to do even when I felt empty and lost.

"Sleep, baby, sleep.
Dream, baby, dream.
Love, baby, love.
My baby, mine."

3

CADEJO IN A CAR

ADELITA

"*D*on't do that. It's creepy."

I don't recognize the man's voice right away. The jostle beneath tells me I'm laying down in moving a car, but the details of how I got here are fuzzy.

There's a hand atop my head. It's warm with a pressure that's comforting, despite my growing worry. I'm either dead, or I'm not dead and have been taken somewhere without my consent.

Maybe I'm in an ambulance. A heavy sigh moves my chest. My eyes are too weighted to open, so I enjoy the hand on my forehead. I let the slight pressure soothe my angst until I'm floating in a sea of "whatever," riding along on the way to the hospital, where surely they know what to do with a stabbed shoulder.

"How long until we get to the hotel?"

Hospital, not hotel. Obviously, that's what he meant to say.

"Not long. Santos, she's alright?" Now I recognize the stern cadence coming from the driver's seat. I bet Cruz looks firm and unemotional still.

My eyes creak open to confirm that no, I'm not in an

ambulance, and no, the three men in jeans and black t-shirts aren't paramedics. My intake of breath alerts the man whose hand is on my forehead that I'm awake.

There were two of them before, yet now in the car there are three.

I take in the sight of a scar-faced man with meek eyes. I don't recognize him, even as he stares down at me with compassion, yet something in the back of my brain rings with the promise of familiarity.

Concern floods his golden irises as his full lips pop open. No sound comes out, but his fussing over my shoulder draws the attention of the other two, who have questions and commands aplenty.

"Adelita, are you in pain?" the man in the passenger's seat asks.

I try to sit up but it's far more effort than I'm used to. The golden-eyed man helps me with a note of reluctance, as if he'd been hoping I'd take up too much of the back seat the entire way to the hospital.

Not hotel. I probably misheard them.

Where's my cardigan? I'm sure it's all bloodied and torn, but I knitted it myself.

He presses a towel to the back of my shoulder, though I don't seem to be actively bleeding anymore. He leans me forward slightly, his hand on my back to keep me from swaying.

My head hurts, but it's second fiddle to the aching scream in my shoulder. "There were men in camo shirts. They hurt Tomás and… Where's Tomás? Is he alright?"

The curly-haired man in the passenger's seat turns his head over his shoulder to give me a blast of his strange eyes —one green and one golden. His brown skin is lighter than the others, and his hair is short on the sides with an inch of curls on top. One of the loops hangs to his eyebrow, making him look too boyish to be wary of. He appears to be a good five years older than me.

He's the one who held down my attacker while Cruz gutted the man.

"Was Tomás the guy in the fetal position? Is that the guy the Kalku attacked?"

My left arm is pretty useless, but my right moves to massage my forehead. "Yes, that's him. Who are the Kalku? Is that like, a gang or something?" Then before he can answer, more questions pop into my brain, spilling out of my mouth like a mess of cards on a bad shuffle. "Who are you? Whose car is this? Where's my car? Is Tomás alright? Which hospital are you taking me to?" Then the most horrifying point of all bursts out of me like a punch. "Did I get stabbed?"

The passenger's seat guy is apparently the only one who's talking to me. He chuckles, of all things. "Which one of those did you want me to answer first?"

"Pick only one," Cruz demands, his eyes on the road. His voice carries a firm command that makes me nervous.

I swallow hard, my shoulder screaming at even that small movement. My pink blouse is drenched in my blood, the sight of which is making me queasy. I guess the knife went all the way through me from back to front. "Alright, let's start with who you all are."

Cruz shakes his head, as if I've failed some secret test. His stern, wider jaw ticks with irritation that looks as if it's engrained throughout his entire being. His voice is gravelly, like he's not had a drink of water in weeks. "Wrong. You should be more concerned about your shoulder. If you bleed out, that's more important than getting our names. Prioritize your needs and you'll get where you need to go."

My lips tighten at being scolded. Mama never talked down to me. She was gentle, which I respond to far better than this *burro* playing mind games in the first minute I'm awake. I don't care if he's correct; right now, all I can think is that he's a jerk.

"Pull over, please."

The man in the passenger's seat rolls his eyes at Cruz. "She was stabbed, dummy. She can ask all the questions she wants."

The wolf. What happened to the sweet, enormous puppy who sat with me while I bled? Is he still guarding Tomás?

"Pull over," I say again, grateful that even though Cruz hasn't learned how to be kind, at least he can follow simple instructions.

When the car comes to a stop on the side of the freeway, I don't bother looking at the golden-eyed man sitting beside me. He's an empath, I can tell, and I don't want us connected through this terrible ordeal.

My stomach twists when I pop the door open. I cannot remember the last time I felt so very comforted as I did when his hand was on my forehead. The second his palm leaves my back, I feel like I'm drifting. And a little like I might bleed out on the highway. "Thanks for the ride, and for showing up when you did. I'll take it from here."

The car jerks forward before I can set my foot on the asphalt. I let out a small shriek when the *pendejo* puts his foot on the gas with such force that the door slams shut on its own.

My shoulder is in agony at being jostled, but when I grab it, that only makes everything worse.

The golden-eyed man moves like he's going to take my offending hand from my wound, but he only mimes the action, so as not to put his hands on me too much when we don't actually know each other.

His expressive eyebrows tent with concern, and for the life of me, I can't help but think how very handsome he is, even with the scarring to the left side of his face. He's got full lips. A mouth like that does me in when it's accompanied by a gentle demeanor that tells me he's never yelled at a woman a day in his life.

Get a grip, girl. That's not the thing to think about when you've been recently stabbed.

I take my hand off my shoulder and use it to grip my knee through the echoes of agony. They're still vibrating through my shoulder and down my arm, protesting the simple movement.

He sits back only when he's convinced that I'm not going to further injure myself by accident. He tucks one of his ink-colored shoulder-length waves behind his ear, revealing high cheekbones that look sculpted by the most skilled artist.

Cruz's voice is sharp but not cruel. "We don't have time for detours. I want to get off the Kalku's radar."

When he turns his chin in my direction, I clearly see bags under his eyes, and a shadow from sleeplessness circling them. He looks strong, gruff and on the edge of haggard. The other two don't look unrested, but it seems Cruz hasn't slept in far too long. His five o'clock shadow is unkempt, which only adds to his unbalanced look.

Just when compassion seeps into my brain, Cruz opens his mouth and ruins it all. "I don't want a fight about us rescuing you and taking you somewhere safe. I want either gratitude or silence. Can you manage either of those?"

I glower up at the back of Cruz's head, noting the short cut of his hair. "I'm not going anywhere with you. Besides, they're both dead. You stabbed the one, and I... Is that what this is about? Because you didn't do anything wrong. It was self-defense. The cops won't nail you for this. You don't need to speed away from the crime scene."

The green-and-gold-eyed man in the passenger's seat takes it upon himself to be the friendly tour guide, since the driver is bullheaded and tightlipped about explaining the things he just said. "I'm Rafael. Next to you is Santos. He's a healer. He got the bleeding to stop in your shoulder and packed it with a salve that'll stave off infection. The blade didn't sever anything too vital, but it's going to take some time to heal. Best be patient and try not to move around too much. It was a Kalku blade, which they always do something manky to. It's not your typical knife wound."

As if I've gotten loads of those, and can run a comparison analysis.

Rafael slaps the driver's bicep. "This is Cruz. He's our fearless leader and terrible communicator." Rafael has a wide smile, and every now and then, one of the curls atop his head bounces with his mannerisms. It's kind of adorable.

I decide I very much like Rafael's casual demeanor. It makes me feel less like I want to jump out of a moving vehicle.

Cruz turns his chin to Rafael with a frown. "Shut up."

Though I've had my most pressing questions answered, another takes their place just as quickly. "How did you know my name?"

Rafael's neck shrinks as he reaches down and lifts my purse from its hiding place at his feet. "We wanted to know who the Kalku thought was important enough to make a grab for. We've been tracking them for quite some time, wondering who they were aiming for next."

"What did they want with Tomás?" I gulp, reaching for my purse with a wince.

Rafael shoots me a wry look, like I'm trying to be funny. "They weren't after your friend. They were aiming to abduct you."

I want to back away from this entire conversation. "I don't know those guys." My brows furrow as my vision focuses in on the man beside me. "Wait, your name is Santos?

There was a wolf back there. You guys called him the same name."

Rafael fixes me with a "duh" stare, like he's waiting for me to figure out the obvious. He's got a current of humor to his movements that endears me to him. Plus, that curly hair begs me to mess it up.

Focus, Adelita.

When I don't have an answer, Rafael jerks his thumb at the scarred man beside me. "Santos is a shapeshifter. A Cadejo. He was the wolf who stayed with you while we fought."

My mouth pops open. The blast of confusion roiling through me is the only thing big enough to distract me from my pain.

When I don't respond, Rafael slows his speech. "Sometimes Santos is a man, and other times, he wants to be a wolf."

I grip my knee as a fresh wave of agony hits my shoulder. "I know what a shapeshifter is, but they're not real."

I meet Santos' eyes and see the same meek golden kindness shining out at me that existed in the wolf. That same feeling of safety that I experienced in the middle of the fray washes through me. It's like his gaze is a hug that holds me when I'm lost.

"They're very real, *linda*. Santos was the wolf who was guarding you."

I don't have anything to say in response to Rafael's declaration that the world is weird and laws of nature are mere suggestions. Well, nothing coherent, that is. I'm torn between running away screaming, coaching them on how to deal with their delusions, and throwing my arms around Santos' neck to thank him for staying with me when it all hit the fan.

Instead of any of those options, I choose to go mute, forfeiting my voice until the world makes sense again.

That is, until Cruz forces too sharp a turn.

"Ah!" Though it's my left shoulder that's injured, my right is also too sore for words, and feels connected to the left. Every movement is tethered to my stab wound.

My stab wound. My stab wound. I've been stabbed.

Santos seems to understand and takes the black bag from Rafael, setting it down between us. He holds up his finger to silently warn me not to stress my injury if I can help it. He hasn't spoken the entire time, but of all three of them, I wish he would. I bet his voice sounds nothing like Cruz's. I bet it's low and soothing, which I wouldn't mind right about now.

Have I seen him before?

No, I would have remembered the scarring. It's literally half his face. Still, I can't shake the feeling that I know this man somehow.

I direct my next words to Santos. "They attacked Tomás, not me. I was only in the mix because I involved myself."

Though as I say this, I wonder how true it is. I'd suspected I was being followed.

My throat is dry as I put the pieces together aloud. "It wouldn't open. My car door. It was stuck so bad, I had to crawl in through the side door. Then when I got out to help Tomás, they acted like I'd passed some sort of initiation rite."

Santos closes his eyes and gives me a sober nod. Why won't he speak to me?

Rafael fills in the gaps. "That's exactly what it was. They're collectors, the Kalku. They're rounding up the exceptional to bring them into their coven."

I squirm in my seat. "Tomás is an exceptional reception-ist. They shouldn't have hurt him like that. Where is he? Did you call an ambulance for him?" I direct my query at Santos, who merely nods once.

Rafael turns fully in his seat and locks eyes with me, letting me know he's not going to tolerate me wiggling out of his polite interrogation. "You know they weren't after Tomás. They only hurt him to lure you into action. That's their way. You have no idea how many scenarios exactly like that one have gone down with very different results in their search for women with special abilities." He pauses for the horrified look on my face, but then presses deeper. "So I have to ask you: why are the Kalku after you? What exceptional quality do you have that they need?"

I bite down on my lower lip and tuck myself into the furthest corner. My heart pounds as the click to my left informs me that Cruz has set the child safety locks in an attempt to seal me inside.

I turn my chin to keep my eyes fixed on the concrete landscape that whips by, resolving to keep my secrets buried for as long as I possibly can.

4

A WOMAN'S HAND

SANTOS

The hotel is your average one-star hole, but for the first time, I'm bothered by our budget-conscious patterns. Obviously Adelita has more refined tastes than this dump.

She's gone completely silent, which I attribute to Cruz, though I can't be mad at him for it. She doesn't see that he was trying to help her by reforming her question. She doesn't understand that teaching someone how to protect themselves is Cruz's version of a hug. Shaken as she is, I think she would prefer an actual embrace.

I miss Eva. Cruz's sister gives great hugs, throwing her arms around you like you're the best thing in the world in that moment. I bet, given some time, Eva would hug Adelita just like that, and give this poor woman the comfort she needs but won't ask for.

Rafael is in the car with her, and every minute that ticks by is one that I worry he's going to charm her with his clever banter. He's got a smile that seems to magnetize women outside of the village to him at first glance. Adelita doesn't need that right now. She was just stabbed. I should be with her since I'm the healer, but Cruz knows I don't have it in me to restrain her if she tries to escape.

But if she does escape, the Kalku will find her and do who knows what to her. They don't understand mercy, only dominance.

"Two rooms, two beds in each. Queens, if you have it." Cruz ignores my frown until the young twenty-something ogling my scars turns to grab us our keys.

Women are always wary of me.

I sign to Cruz that Adelita won't want to share a room with a stranger, which is exactly what we are to her.

Cruz mutters in my direction. "I don't care if she's not going to be happy about sharing a room. She'll be safe, which is the important thing. I'll even let her pick who she shares a room with, if that helps you."

I'm surprised he's giving her that much tether. Usually Cruz is more controlling than that.

Cruz's face sours. "Scratch that. I don't want Rafael trying to seduce her."

That's more like Cruz, thinking things through to examine all the holes.

The receptionist throws him a flirty smile. She's cute, no doubt about it, but Cruz couldn't care less. She could be naked and throw herself at his feet, and he wouldn't dare take her home. Too dangerous. Plus, different worlds and all that. Though, Cruz decides to be gracious and rewards her interest in him with a modest nod devoid of a smile.

On our way back to the car, Cruz cuts with no finesse. "You up for guarding Adelita tonight? I have to sleep, so I know it can't be me."

I nod once. I've got a new patient who's been stabbed. I want to tell Cruz that I'll be staying with Adelita until her shoulder is healed, but I sense we've taken away enough of Adelita's choices in life. She probably wouldn't take kindly to my hovering.

Cruz is nervous. I can tell by the way he fiddles with his keys in his jacket pocket. He thinks by appearing stoic he covers all his tells, but in the two-and-a-half years I've known him, he has a myriad of signals he doesn't realize he gives off.

We need to figure out why the Kalku want her, but unlike the last two we rescued, she's tight-lipped. Whatever heightened ability she has, it must be bad.

Or we must've blown the whole "the truth is out there" speech so horribly that she wouldn't tell us even her greatest talent was being able to perform a somersault.

When we get into the car, we interrupt her quiet laughter. It guts me a little bit that Rafael is so charming; he's already found a way to make her smile.

Cruz slices through the merriment with his steely edict. "I got us two rooms around back. We can stay here for a day or so until we figure out our next move."

What he means to say is "we're keeping you hidden until you tell us why the Kalku are targeting you," but kudos to Cruz for not coming out and saying something so asinine.

Cruz shoves his keys into the ignition and drives slowly around to the back of the building. "Someone has to stay with you, Adelita. If the Kalku got to you once, they won't stop until they have you. Whatever it is you can do, they need it."

Rafael translates. "The good news is that if one of us is with you, you're safe. The bad news is that one of us has to be with you at all times. Pick your poison, *linda*."

She smirks at the impromptu term of endearment. Rafael always gets away with stuff like that. He's good at making people feel at ease.

Leave it to Cruz to put a damper on her burgeoning smile. "No. Santos can guard you. Rafi, we don't need this one going the way of the last few we rescued." His eyes flick to hers after he parks the car at the rear of the building. He turns off the ignition and shoves open his door.

Rafael takes the verbal chastisement in stride, casting Adelita an exaggerated look of disappointment before he exits the vehicle. "Looks like you're going to have to cry yourself to sleep because you miss me so much. I'll be in the next room if you need me."

"I'll keep that in mind." She's not flirty or giggly with him.

Even so, Rafael is a professional at relaxing anyone he talks to for five seconds.

Her movements are tight with pain and nerves. I only exit the car once she does. My eyes track her movements for signals of distress she's not comfortable voicing.

She narrows her eyes at us. "I really don't need a chaperone."

Cruz doesn't pull punches, though every now and then, I wish he would. "It's not for you to decide what you need right now. You don't know anything about the Kalku. We do. They're targeting you, and you won't tell us why. Until we better understand what we're dealing with, one of us is with you at all times."

She harrumphs, and I'm certain I've never seen anything more fascinating than Adelita when she gets riled up. Her eyes tell him off in a dozen ways while her lips remain pursed through her indignation.

She reins in her words with a cool, "Not for nothing, but I have work in the morning. I'm not staying in a hotel with you. I need to go to the hospital. I've been stabbed, in case that's escaped your notice."

Cruz's jaw is firm. "I wasn't about to offer staying with me as an option." His tone is so caustic that I wince on her behalf. "You'll stay in the room with Santos. He's the better choice anyway. He's the one who got your shoulder to stop bleeding. He's the one who made sure infection didn't set in. He's the reason you don't actually need to go to the hospital."

I fully expect her to wilt under Cruz's harsh demeanor, but she stiffens, holding her own. "Are you the reason I don't get to go to my home? I mean, if I'm fine and all, thanks to Santos, then I should be able to go. Am I your prisoner? Are you holding me hostage?"

Cruz's lips tighten.

The other rescue victims didn't exactly warm to him, but they didn't talk back this much either. Usually women outside of our tribe throw themselves at him before he turns them off with his personality. Then they clam up around him, which I'm sure is how he prefers it. He doesn't like explaining himself or his plans. He wants soldiers, and is used to being revered.

I rather enjoy seeing Cruz flummoxed. His nostrils flare three times before he answers.

"You'd be a prisoner with a shortened lifespan if the Kalku got their hands on you. If we hadn't intervened, they would've taken you already. I trust you're smart enough not to want that."

Her eyes are big, and I can see plainly her debate between fear and bravery.

I've never seen blue eyes before. Hers are mesmerizing.

How Cruz can stare so coldly under the weight of those beautiful eyes is beyond me.

"Why do they want me?"

She's doing it again, saying thirty things with her eyes while she shuts her lips tight after a single sentence. She operates with an intensity that captures my attention like nothing else.

Cruz holds her gaze for one whole beat before he has to

look away from the raw emotion she radiates. "They're collectors. Nothing more complicated than that. The fact that they're gunning for you? Only you know the answer to that. The sooner you tell us, the better we'll be able to protect you from them."

Three seconds is all Rafi can be expected to hold back. He closes the gap between them and places his hand on the small of her back.

It's that little touch and the fact that she doesn't jerk away that seals it.

She'll be like the others and fall into his bed. I don't begrudge him his flirtatious exchanges, but for some reason, I wish he'd hold himself back from this one. The others hadn't been stabbed.

Adelita is an outsider, and we're expecting her to keep up with no explanations.

"What if I don't need protection?" she says quietly. I can tell it's not defiance speaking, but nerves. She's on the cusp of confessing her secret that drew the Kalku in, I can feel it. I lean in, but at Cruz's scoff, I see her clamming up once more.

Cruz misunderstands, as is often his way. He comes down hard on her while I fetch the bags from the trunk. "If that were true, we wouldn't have been picking you up off the concrete, unconscious, after slaughtering the Kalku so you could escape. Like it or not, you need us. You have no idea what you're dealing with. You didn't even know you were being watched." He turns his attention to me. "Santos, you need to show her. She hasn't seen you shift. Let her get used to you here."

I don't want her to be afraid of me. By some strange twist of fate, I might be the one she's least afraid of, which is a first for me, for sure. Back at the village, they call me Santos the Savage. I don't want to push her in that direction.

But I don't disobey. Cruz gave me a directive, so after

glancing around to make sure no one is around to see it, I comply. I tense up my abdomen and picture my wolf before I blow out my humanity in a long breath.

When I start the breath, I'm a man. When I finish, I'm a wolf, standing on all fours in front of her, afraid to look up. I don't want to see her fear. It pierces me more than it should, and I really don't want to be the cause of it.

She yelps and jumps back, but that seems to be the worst of it. I don't expect her to step toward me with a tentative shuffle. I don't know what to do with myself when she kneels down before me after a few beats, putting herself on my level.

I don't focus on the confusion; the longing in her eyes is too strong for me to make out the specifics of her worry.

It's not until she addresses me, instead of Cruz, that I see the bravery there behind the concern. "Can I pet you? Do you still know who I am?"

I nod, careful when I step toward her. I lower my head in an act of submission so she can do with me as she pleases.

There is nothing better than a woman's hand combing through my fur. It's one of the luxuries life rarely grants me, yet somehow today is my luckiest of days.

Adelita's fingers are soft, making me wish my fur was something nicer to present to her. If my human face scares people, my wolf body is even worse. Scars on my animal take away whole chunks of my fur, making me look rabid and wild. I don't get the chance to assure the villagers that I'm tame before they're shirking away, moving to the opposite end of the street whenever I pass by.

But even in the middle of a knife fight, Adelita saw me. She looked past my scars and made the decision that I'm not a menace she should fear.

I don't even realize I'm laying down until she coos. Suddenly, I'm her puppy, and my only job is to let her dote on me. I rest my maw on her thigh to show her I trust her touch, and she responds by scratching under my chin.

I love this woman. I can't help myself. Whatever love is, I feel it now, caressing my insides in time with her soothing touch.

"Well, that's new," Rafi comments.

And just like that, the mood is broken.

As if she's just now realizing I'm a man, and this is a new bit of magic she doesn't understand, she lets loose a nervous chuckle. "Sorry. I guess I'm a little out of my depth here. It's okay that I pet you?"

I respond by running my head under her hand to tell her that's exactly where she belongs. I'll keep her safe. If she prefers me in this form, that's fine.

Rafael folds his arms over his chest. "So we can move past the 'shapeshifters don't exist' portion of the evening?"

She nods and I see her wince. She needs to lie down. She needs iron from all her blood loss. I'm sure she'd like a shower and some clean clothes.

Rafael helps her to stand, rephrasing Cruz's edict in a more palatable fashion. "The Kalku are tracking you, even now. Once they lock their focus on someone, they don't stop until they have you. We've been rescuing the women they abduct for years." He's calm in the way he delivers the truth, and I can see she's finally starting to hear it. "Trust me, you don't want to be someone they catch. If it's okay with you, we can hide out here tonight. Santos can fix up your shoulder, and we'll make sure no one comes after you tonight." His smile quirks to the side. "That okay?"

I can tell she wants to argue every single one of his points, but eventually, she deflates at Rafi's logic. "I guess that's fair. I'll stay one night, and then we'll go to the police in the morning."

I need to look at her shoulder. I tighten my abdomen and

suck in my breath as I picture my man form. By the time the air is collected into my lungs, I've spooked her by transforming without warning.

I hold up my hands to prove I'm not going to hurt her, and she exhales with a nervous chuckle. Then her lashes flutter, and I can tell she's struggling to stay upright.

Cruz narrows his eyes at her, cutting her no slack to adjust to the learning curve that comes when a new world is introduced to a person. "The Kalku don't answer to the police. The second they see you go back to your normal routine, they'll pounce. If you escaped two Kalku members before, the next time they'll send a flood of them. Whatever you can do, they want you in their cave. They're not going to stop until you're captured."

They're all the wrong words, but as she bites down on her lower lip, I can see it inflicts the desired fear that will keep her from running. At least, I hope that's what she hears.

Cruz is terrible at people.

"Cave? Captured?"

When a swoon hits her, I don't think anything through. I drop the bags and dash to her side, dodging Rafi as I scoop her up. She groans through the jostle to her shoulder, but she's too weak to protest much more.

It's decided. I will stay with her. She needs rest. She needs iron. She needs someone other than Cruz explaining things to her. And she really, really doesn't need Rafael's hand on her back.

Rafi usually hugs me before we go to sleep, but he settles for a kiss to my cheek instead tonight.

Adelita is awake enough that she could protest if she wanted to, but she doesn't. She doesn't look afraid of me or my scars, which is a first for me. She doesn't struggle out of my grip at all as I lead the way to the hotel room and shut us inside, leaving Cruz and Rafael to sort out their evening away from her.

5

SCALES AND SCARS
SANTOS

I hate this. I hate my curse. I'm scaring her by not speaking, but some things just can't be helped. I know she probably doesn't want me anywhere near her bed but I lay her on it anyway, making it clear that I'm taking the one nearest the door, and she gets the bed nearer the bathroom.

"I don't feel well," she admits, now that it's just us.

It's a great relief that she's confessing this small bit of obvious news to me. If she can speak candidly about her physical pain, the internal wounds will soon come to light. Then perhaps she'll tell me why the Kalku came after her. Only then will we know what we're dealing with.

I pull a chair from the desk in the corner up to her bedside and hold her left hand. It's to show solidarity, sure, but also it helps me gage her pain and reflexes.

Slowly, I turn her wrist, taking note of her features when the pain registers on her face. I lift her elbow an inch, but that's all the movement I'll allow.

I touch my stomach, hoping she understands that I'm asking her if her abdomen hurts.

"No. It's just my shoulder. And my head a little."

I take my time prodding her skull to check for lumps or abrasions. There's a tender spot on the back of her head that makes her wince when I lightly touch it.

"Santos, do you have a medical degree?"

She's lucid enough to fix me with her bright blue eyes, which is a good thing. It means her headache will clear eventually. There wasn't a concussion to further damage things.

I give her a slow shake of my head, though I know this will only worry her more. I've stitched up hundreds of knife wounds and none of my patients ever fell to infection.

Still, I know how I must look to her.

Santos the Savage.

Her jaw sets with determination. "I should go to a hospital."

I realize now I've shut out Rafi too soon. She needs someone who can explain this all to her. Even Cruz would be a better option than me at this point.

I hold up my finger and trot to the next room, motioning for Rafael to help me out.

"She's still insisting we take her to a hospital. Explain it to her?"

Rafi studies the flashing movements of my fingers before slapping me on the shoulder. "She needs me, eh? Can't say I'm surprised."

I swallow my glower and lead him back to Adelita, who makes an effort to sit up at the company.

I hold out my hands to tell her that this isn't the time to move around.

"Why can't I go to the hospital? I was just stabbed! I'm really trying not to freak out but you're not giving me much to work with. You can keep me away from the Kalku in the hospital, right?"

Rafael sits on the edge of her bed like it's no big thing. I wish I had the gumption to do something bold like that.

Adelita doesn't seem bothered at all to have Rafi in her space.

"Adelita, Adelita. It's been a long day for you, *linda*. Santos is the best healer there is, and he's not going to leave your side until your shoulder's well enough to punch Cruz in the face the next time he says something stupid. See this?" He lifts up his shirt, I'm positive, just to show off his hard-earned musculature. He takes her finger and puts it on his scar as if she's blind and needs to feel her way through life. "That's from the Kalku. Santos here patched me up, and I'm good as new. See these?" He turns his back to her and displays several dime-sized scars on the right side of his spine. "Those are from a dustup with the Kalku. Santos dug out every single last piece. Didn't use anesthetic on me, the jerk. You're lucky he likes you. He numbed your shoulder before going to town on that wound of yours."

"No anesthesia?"

Rafi laughs like it's all hilarious. "Yeah. It was to teach me a lesson, since the Kalku only found us because of my mistake. Point is, Santos knows what he's doing. He's better than a hospital. The Kalku can find you in a hospital. Their man stabbed you the second he saw us coming. He wanted to ensure that, if you got away, he'd be able to track you down by checking the hospital. You're hidden here with us."

She relaxes into the pillow, and I breathe a little easier. "So this Kalku group… Bad guys, eh?"

"Very bad guys, yes."

"And you?" she asks. "Are you a bad guy?"

It's a simple question, not laced with judgment. She's being kidnapped by us, for lack of a better term. She wants to know who she's dealing with, and how worried she should be.

Rafi tilts his head at her, his mouth drawing to the side. "I think that's for you to decide. But if you're worried we'll hurt you, I can assure you that we won't. In fact, we haven't done a thing but get you to safety and patch you up. Even if our version of a rescue isn't the same as yours, perhaps it's good enough to get you to stop worrying we're going to turn and attack you."

Rafael is bold enough to brush a stray midnight-colored wave from her forehead and tuck it behind her ear. He's flirting, but he's also testing the trust between them. I watch with fascination, taking note of how normal people go about this sort of thing.

One day, I'll be normal.

She allows him to touch her face. She lets him prove to her that he's not going to harm her.

Adelita purses her lips. "Why did they try to take me?"

"You stood out to them. The question is why. Only you know the answer to that. They take all sorts of people they think are valuable. Trust me when I say that you don't want to know what it's like once they've got you." Pain flickers in Rafael's eyes, and I know he's remembering too much. I'm sure he'll never forget the things the elders promised would fade with age. One day, those childhood memories won't haunt him.

Of course she doesn't answer him. That would be too simple. Instead she bites on her lower lip and I lean in, nearly losing myself to the desire to touch that plump bit of flesh she's gambling our entire mission on. "Did they take you?"

My sharp inhale draws her eyes, but they tether back to Rafael, who looks as if she's just flayed him wide open with her astute observation.

Rafi nods slowly, and I think for a moment he's going to leave it at that. No one asks him to talk about it all because everyone in our tribe already understands. They know better than to ask about his time in the caves of the Kalku, but she doesn't. She steps on his well-placed landmine, but she does it with such innocence that Rafael can't be angry.

With the way her doe eyes blink at him, I'd be shocked if anyone's raised their voice to her ever.

Rafi's reply has a forced steadiness to it. "They stole me as a baby, but I was lucky. I was rescued when I was five years old. It could have been much worse for me. Santos wasn't rescued until two or three years ago." He points to his eyes. "They started the process of turning me into an imbunche and a shapeshifter, but I was liberated before they could complete the process. So I can half-change, but that's it. Still, it's enough to scare everyone who knows anything about our world."

She touches her pursed lips, muscling past the knee-jerk denial as she drinks it all in. "Can you show me? I want to know what a half-wolf looks like, so I can recognize you. I don't think I want to be afraid of you."

To his credit, Rafi puts on a casual smile as if the whole thing hasn't wrecked his life. "Sure, *linda*. But I'm not a wolf. My animal took the form of a dragon, but never came full-circle."

He steps to the side and draws in the breath I've coached him through. He'd never been able to get this far until I joined them. He only breathed a few sparks on occasion. Still, after two years of working with him, all I've managed to bring out is a man with a forked tail, covered in olive scales with gold tips from head to toe.

She yelps at the transformation, shirking away with her hand over her mouth. "Oh, Rafael! I... This is..." I can see fear in her eyes that melts to sadness. Then compassion rises, pushing out the angst of seeing something so foreign. She stumbles through too many half-reactions before finally settling on curiosity. "Can I... Would it be okay if I touched your scales?"

Always the charmer, Rafi tilts his head to the side like he expects her to want to come nearer, though no woman ever has. I truly don't understand how he's managed to hold on to his cockiness. Everyone in the village is disgusted by us, calling us monsters because we've been genetically altered. As if we somehow don't still have access to our human brains when we've transitioned.

Rafael holds out his hand, letting her touch the smallest parts of him so she doesn't have to come too near.

But Adelita is a searcher. With much effort, she sits up and leans forward, away from her fear, and runs her hand up Rafael's forearm all the way to his bicep.

Just like how the hairs on a person's arm stand up when they're overexcited, Rafael's scales stiffen and the golden tips lift up through his shiver.

"They're so hard but still flexible. Like a strange kind of rubber. Does this hurt?" she asks as she slides her finger under one of his scales. Each one is the size of a guitar pick.

Rafael's eyes close as a wave of pleasure visibly rocks through him. "That feels amazing. All of it. It only hurts if I snap off a scale."

"What happens if you break one off?"

"Feels like breaking a finger. It grows back eventually, but it's not pleasant." Though she hasn't asked all that many questions, Rafi volunteers information. "We heal faster than average—Santos and me."

She's encroaching on his body space now, her chest just two inches from his. I'm frozen at the sight, debating between wanting to cheer for Rafael's victory in getting a woman to come near, and also wanting to shove him away so she pets only me.

Rafael shivers when her hand caresses his chest.

She retracts her touch, as if only just remembering that

he's still a man, not just a half-dragon. "Sorry. I probably shouldn't have done that."

He sucks in his breath and the scales vanish, leaving him in his man form. A relaxed grin settles on his features, his shoulders rolled back. "Never stop touching me just like that. Do you know how rare it is any woman comes near me or Santos? Because we can mutate like that, the villagers don't want anything to do with us. Unless they need protecting. Then we're pushed to the front lines to take all the hits for them. Put the mutants in danger, right? They're not whole-humans, so they don't matter as much."

Her hand flies over her heart. "That's awful!"

True hurt bleeds through his words. "They call us monsters."

Her brows lower in what looks like indignation. "Mama used to say that monsters are what you make of them."

Rafi jerks his chin at her. "If that's true, then what do you make of us?"

She glances from Rafi to me, and back again. "I think you rescued me."

Rafi's smirk draws up on the left side of his face. "I knew I liked you, *linda*."

I don't want him talking about my life. It's private, and she doesn't need the details.

I sign as much to him, and Adelita's mouth falls open. "You're deaf?" No doubt she's just now realizing I haven't spoken a word this entire time. It's amazing how long I can go before people make that connection.

I shake my head but Rafi takes up the mantle and explains for me.

I don't want to hear it. The whole story makes me sick to my stomach.

Twin brothers taken by the Kalku at birth.

Years later, Cruz and his men show up to liberate the captives but only manage to free one of the twins.

Before I could be freed, I was cursed with silence.

As if that's the worst thing you can do to a man.

Killing a man's brother. That's the worst thing you can do to him. To keep my twin from being liberated, they murdered him. Murdered their own slave, while I was set free, yet confined to silence.

Rafi gives her the cleaned-up version. "Santos isn't deaf; he's been cursed. The Kalku are a group of wicked people who deal in curses. Cruz and I rescued Santos, but before we could get him out, they took away his right to speak. Do you know how they do that?"

She shakes her head and then turns her chin to me.

It steals the air from my lungs when I see her eyes are wet. One blink, and there they go, a line of emotion bleeding down her cheek.

She didn't cry when she was stabbed. She didn't weep when she realized we were politely abducting her. But now she's upset because something bad happened to a man she doesn't even really know? A savage?

"They took away your voice?"

I nod once, but that's all I'm capable of. I'm not used to being so near crying women. Being that we're always on the road tracking the Kalku soldiers, I'm not used to being around women, period.

I can't... I don't like this. I'm torn between wanting to grab her a tissue and needing to bolt out of the room.

She reaches her hand toward me in a show of kindness, but her face pulls at the motion she really shouldn't be doing.

Just like that, I'm myself again. I may not know how to be around women, but I know how to treat a stab wound.

I move over to my bed and yank the sheet from underneath the comforter. I keep my eyes on my knife as I cut several four-inch long strips and fashion them into a sling while Rafael tells her highlights of my sad story.

"The Kalku's curses take the physical form of an axe. They conjure up a curse, and a golden axe appears in a curse tree somewhere in the world. It's usually engraved with a picture of what the curse will do, too. Once the axe appears in the tree, there it stays. As long as the axe is embedded in the tree, the curse stands."

"Why don't you just remove the axe?"

Rafael's lopsided smile is gentle with her logical, if not naïve, question. "The axe is bound so it can't be removed, except by the person who crafted the curse. We've tried everything on many different curse axes. Tied it to our car, and it still stayed stuck. Tried cutting down the tree itself, but the whole trunk is made more solid by the curse running through it. So for now, we don't know how to free Santos from his curse of muteness, or any of the other cursed people from their afflictions, for that matter. But we don't lose hope. If something can be done, it can be undone as well. That's one of the cardinal rules of magic."

"Magic," she echoes, as if tasting the word to see if it's laced with poison or some kind of trap.

I probably don't have to stand behind her to drape the fabric over her shoulder, but if she looks into my eyes with those tears again, I know I'll bolt out the door.

So I hide in plain sight.

It's not until Rafi reaches forward and thumbs at one of the droplets that I feel a brand of frustration I'm not sure I've ever entertained.

I've never begrudged Rafael anything. Whatever trinket catches his eye, I do my utmost to secure for him. Same goes for Cruz. When they rescued me from enslavement, their missions became mine. Their people, my own. It's the least I can do. I owe them every day of my freedom, and they've never taken advantage of my loyalty.

When Rafael brushes Adelita's other cheek with his knuckle, it's all for indulgence. There aren't even any tears there.

He glances up at me standing behind her as I cinch the sling around her arm. He flinches at the sight of me. He recoils and holds both hands up in surrender.

It's not until then I realize the coldness of my glare and the curl of my upper lip. I manage to brush the malice off my face before Adelita catches my moment of weakness.

I don't know what's gotten into me. Rafi is my family. My adoptive brother. My friend. I shouldn't act like this.

Rafael steps back to give the bed a healthy three feet of space. "Santos is a good man. You don't have to worry about a thing with him. He was the healer for the Kalku, back when he was enslaved. Now that Santos is free, he's chosen what kind of man he wants to be. He's devoted his life to helping Cruz take down the Kalku."

She's taking it all in, and I'm worried about how it's tumbling around inside of her. I don't want her to think I'm scary or savage.

"'Evil needs only permission to thrive,'" she says solemnly. "My mom used to say that. It sounds like you three are firm that the evil will be stopped. I like that."

When she turns to trap me in her eyeline, I trot to the bathroom to wash my hands. I'm sure it looks like I'm being professional, but really, I'm scared of that look in her eyes. She wears an unbridled care for strangers I'd dismissed as myth a long time ago. No one cared that I'd gone missing as a baby. No one came looking for my brother and me. Only Cruz and Rafi came searching, and they hadn't even been looking specifically for me, but for prisoners.

When I come out, she's telling Rafael goodnight and staring at me with more purpose this time than worry.

She waits until the door closes us in the motel room together before she blurts out, "Are you and your brother identical twins?"

Of all the things I think she'll say to me, that one didn't make the list. I give her a simple nod and an inquiring eyebrow. Her tears are wiped clean, but worse than compassion, there's now fear tightening her mouth.

She doesn't explain herself, but clears the gap between us, shocking me when she lifts her right hand to cover half of my face.

She's not hiding my scars from view to be cruel, I don't think. She's too scared for that. She wants to use her left hand, but the sling keeps her from hurting herself.

Her touch is… It's heady to be touched by a woman. Any man who thinks otherwise is spoiled by good luck. Women are mostly frightened of either my upbringing or my scars, so they don't come near.

I have to remind my heart not to hammer too loudly. My whole body freezes as panic hits my nervous system.

Am I supposed to touch her face? Should I lean in to the touch? I don't want it to end. Why is she looking at me with such intensity? Is this friendship? Is this what Rafael does with women when he gets them alone in the motel room?

Her voice is quiet, but the air is so thick with intensity that the sound is amplified in my ears. "Will you sit for a second? I need to see something."

I do as she asks because honestly, aside from requesting to be let go, she's asked for nothing. She's standing before me in a torn and bloodied shirt, but she hasn't even asked for a new one.

She fishes the two-inch clip from her hair and holds it

between her teeth. "I'm sorry, I just... I have to see something."

My vertebrae melt in a slow line down my back when she combs her fingernails through the hair on the right side of my head. I can't feign stoicism as my eyes close. I want to savor what it feels like to be touched this way by a woman. Her fingers are silk as they direct the turn of my chin. My body trusts her for no reason other than pure instinct.

My eyes flash open at the snap of her clip securing part of my hair back from my face. My hair isn't too long, not as long as my brother's was. Mine only falls to my chin, where Santiago's touched his shoulders.

She moves to my right side as if she's seeing a ghost. She steps back and covers her mouth, and I worry I've suddenly done something to frighten her. "Santiago!"

Of all the things I expect her to say, my dead twin brother's name, whom she's never met, stuns my heart into a rapid race.

6

GOING TOO FAR
CRUZ

J have never shopped for women's clothing before. I rarely buy new clothes for myself. If something tears, Santos sews it. Most of my shirts have seen a fair amount of bloodshed, which is why the guys and I wear black. But this woman in her pink silky blouse stands out like a flashing warning light. Maybe if she puts on this black shirt, like the rest of us, my eyes will stop zinging to her.

I need to know why the Kalku thinks she's useful. She doesn't seem like she secretly belongs to any of the tribes who know about the real way the world works. Still, I've been fooled before, so I try to keep a tight tether on everything surrounding her, just in case I'm wrong.

Man, I hate being wrong.

But my gut tells me she's completely in the dark as to what all this mess might mean for her. She certainly didn't look fearsome, or like she'd been expecting the Kalku to attack. She hadn't been armed, nor had she called anyone to come to her aid.

Come to think of it, she hasn't asked us to call anyone to even let them know she was missing. I can't decide if that's suspicious or sad. I'm too tired to puzzle her out right now. Though, I'm always too tired for just about anything.

Rafael moved my driver's license to the back slot in my wallet. He knows I hate when he messes with my stuff, but he does it anyway just to entertain himself.

Annoying.

I keep my head down while I walk, though the Kalku can spot me easily enough. I'm too tall to be stealthy, and too recognizable by anyone from all three of the tribes to pass through anywhere incognito.

Luckily, we're out in the normal world, where most of our tribe doesn't care to venture.

I circle the area three times to make sure I'm not being followed before I trot toward the motel room. Standing outside Adelita's door, I suddenly feel guilty about waking her if she's asleep.

I run my hand through my hair, as if I'm getting ready for some big ceremony or presentation I have to give in front of the village.

Pulling my hand away, I stare at it in confusion. What should it matter if my hair is in place?

This whole traveling with a woman thing is playing tricks on my mind. The other rescues were easy enough to ignore because Rafi proved a nice distraction for them.

I knock four times in a pattern the three of us know. *Rat rat-a-tat.* I'm expecting Santos to greet me with lidded eyes. We've been on the road for weeks, and don't always take the time to stretch out in motel beds.

When the door flings open and Santos meets my gaze with wild eyes, fresh fear on his face and half his hair pulled back in a pink clip, my stomach sinks. "Why didn't you text me? Is something wrong with her? You told me the stab wound would heal fine." I push past him, anticipating the worst.

Adelita dead on the mattress.

Adelita's big blue eyes open in a silent plea for me to stop being stubborn and take her to the Emergency Room.

But she's not dead. She's tucked herself into the far corner of the quaint room, looking just as scared as Santos.

"What is it? What happened?" I draw my knife on instinct. Santos is spooked by something, that's for sure.

"She knows him," he signs. *"Adelita knows Santiago!"*

Santos' sign for "Adelita" is an "A" mixed with the sign for "beautiful." I don't know why this catches me off-guard. Usually he uses some non-opinionated physical attribute. His sign for me is a "C" next to an exaggerated scowl. His sign for Rafael is an "R" near his crotch because, well, it's Rafi. There's no opinion in those, only fact. Rafi thinks with his dick, and I look like... well, whatever the opposite of the Easter Bunny looks like.

But Santos thinks Adelita is beautiful. I can't disagree, but I also can't think of a scenario in which Santos getting hung up on a woman the Kalku are after might be considered a good thing. She is pretty. Heart-shaped face with a sun-kissed umber to her skin. Pink lips that are the right amount of full. Blue eyes that make me forget everything else in the world.

My brain snaps into focus. I must be tired if the main point of Santos' message blew past me.

My head whips to Adelita. She looks like a scared child who just broke her grandmother's tea cup by mistake. "How do you know Santiago? The Kalku kept him locked up tight before they killed him. He was in captivity from the time he was a baby."

Her eyes are huge with worry.

"Tell me, Adelita!"

She jumps at the bark in my voice. Normally, I enjoy the way my military-bred commands invoke fear, but I don't like the look of her distress. It turns my stomach, especially since I'm the cause of it. My sister always tells me I have no idea how to speak to women, but I brushed that off until Eva's words come shouting back at me in Adelita's distrusting eyes.

Rafi strolls in and shuts the door behind him. His shoulders are rolled back as if my frustration is amusing. "What seems to be the problem, kids? I heard yelling through the wall. That means we're dealing with either really thin walls, or someone put his cranky pants on tonight." He shoots me an exaggerated frown.

I set the bag of clothes down on the bed and fix Adelita with a cold stare. "You will confess how you know Santiago, or I'll have no choice but to assume you're in league with the Kalku."

She remains mute, though now I can see it's mainly from stubbornness. I didn't say "please" or keep my tone at the cheery level of an elementary school teacher, so she's digging her heels in when I need her honest and open.

Rafi sizes up the tenor of the room with a lackadaisical shrug. "Tell me, oh fearless leader, how Adelita might be in league with the Kalku? They were trying to kill her."

"They let her escape!" I counter.

"With a knife wound?"

"A knife wound that left her alive."

Rafi gives me a steady stare that lets me know I'm being stupid. "That's a fairly convincing bit of acting they pulled off. Were they faking their own deaths at our hands, too? What would her motive be for letting us take her with us if she was really part of the Kalku? And since when have you known them to let women into their fold? They use them, sure, but they don't give them instrumental roles like enemy infiltration."

I throw my hands up. "How else do you explain her knowing Santiago?"

Rafi's tone is irritatingly calm and patronizing. "Well, I don't know. Perhaps we should yell at her and hope that gets us closer to some answers."

Santos sits on the edge of the bed, pinching the bridge of his nose while we all try to puzzle this out.

I fix my eyes on Adelita, who visibly recoils, shoving herself further into the corner, as if she's hoping the shadows might swallow her whole. "I will get the information from you," I warn her, silently begging her to tell me the truth. "It's up to you how long that takes."

Rafi tenses, but perhaps he trusts that I won't use force to extract the information I need, like I usually resort to. He doesn't move to stop me, but watches my conscience give a rousing fight against the mission that remains at the fore-front of my mind: I must take down the Kalku at all costs. Nothing else matters.

I hate this. My stomach churns as I step toward Adelita. "How do you know Santiago?"

She's as mute as Santos, who's still stuck mid-consternation from his perch on the bed.

"Tell me now, or I will hurt you." I'm warning her because I don't want to. I want her to stop me.

Santos' head whips up while Rafi's eyes track my every move.

I don't stop until I've got her trapped in the corner, hemmed in by my intimidating form. It was her choice to escape to this spot but it'll be my choice if she is permitted to leave it. My bulk fills her vision, her sharp inhale bracing herself against my very presence.

When she opens her mouth, I'm relieved that I won't have to lay a hand on her, until the words spit out at me so quiet, I nearly lose my resolve. "Is this the man you want to be?"

Her words dig into me, unearthing anger, shame and worst of all, concern.

Am I the man I set out to be? Is this how I saw my life going? Cornering a woman because she's too scared to answer my questions?

I purse my lips and steel myself against Adelita's eyes that seem to see right through me. "I am the man I have to be."

Her voice is filled with pity and emotion. "Then I am sorry for you."

My thumb doesn't even have to press all that hard into her shoulder to make her scream. New wounds are funny like that.

I don't let up, even as Rafi tugs on my elbow. "Enough, Cruz! This isn't the way. You'll make her bleed all over again. Get off her!"

Rafi is strong but I'm a tank. "Tell me how you know Santiago!"

I don't have to look outside to know a fog is moving through the area. That's what you get when you're tied to the weather.

The man I set out to be was my father—who only influences the weather when something catastrophic happens to the village. Yet here I am, going off-book because I can't see any other way to get the job done. And nature is tattling on me, matching the clouds to my mood to tell the world that I'm confused and upset.

Adelita jerks against the wall as pain shoots through her, but she's not fighting back. In fact, she's gritting her teeth in what looks like determination not to raise a hand to push me away. Not like it would do any good, but still, this woman has no idea how to defend herself. She looks like she's afraid to even try.

Her wound is warm and seeps fresh blood through the stained silk of her pink shirt. She's choking on her breath, each inhale alerting her to more pain that would all go away if only she would talk.

I add more pressure, twisting my thumb and tearing open the stitches. Santos will no doubt be annoyed I ripped open his handiwork. Her screams shoot straight into my stomach, shredding me without laying a finger to inflict the pain we both know I deserve.

She's sweating, and I worry I'm hurting her worse than simple pain. Can her body handle distress like this? I don't know anything about her.

Rafi finally rips me away from her but it's not in time. Adelita's knees buckle, and for the second time, she passes clean out.

Dread washes cold regret through me.

Rafi's pissed, which is a strange color on him, to be sure. "Enough! Not like this, Cruz. Never like this. We saved her for what? So you could torture her? What protection has the Cáceres tribe offered her now? A roof over her head only if she lets you maim her?" Then something to his left catches his eye and he cries out. "Santos, no!"

I shake him off, but he's already darting toward the side of the room. His words are a steady stream of profanity as he drops to his knees beside Santos, who's rocking himself maniacally on the threadbare carpet.

I hate when Santos gets lost like this. He's hugging his midsection and rocking back and forth on his knees. His eyes are wide in a silent scream that can't find its way to his lips.

Worse is the dagger sticking out of his thigh. Blood's been pooling on the carpet for who knows how many seconds, manifesting agony he can't express any other way.

"Do you see what you did?" Rafi yells at me, shoving me hard before he drops to his knees in front of Santos. Rafi grips the back of Santos' head, threading his fingers through his hair as he brings Santos forward to rest his forehead on

Rafi's shoulder. "Shh," he whispers in a paternal voice to Santos.

Though Santos can't speak, the angst roiling around inside of him is loud.

I did this. I made a woman faint. I made a woman bleed. I made Santos so crazy that he drove his own dagger into his thigh.

I wonder how long ago it was that I lost myself.

No, I am not the man I set out to become.

"You did this!" Rafi shouts.

Most think he's a clown, always joking around without any real compass. Rafi doesn't get pushed to the edge all too often, but when he does, he's a force to be reckoned with.

"Santos won't correct you because you saved him from the Kalku. He won't stop you from hurting the woman he just saved because he trusts that you always do the right thing. But this is wrong, Cruz! You're way off the map on this. So Adelita knows Santiago. What does that prove? If she was in league with the Kalku, she wouldn't have been stupid enough to tell Santos she knew anything about Santiago! They wouldn't have attacked her! Use your head!"

I cast around for all my reasons that were so clear to me mere seconds ago. I can't think when Santos is bleeding. I can't see past the ruby puddle marking this as the spot where I lost my hold on the man I was supposed to be, and turned into my father's brother. Tio Bruno would be proud, which is the biggest red flag of all.

Rafi is on his knees, gripping the back of Santos' head while his other hand drifts down to coil around the hilt of the dagger. "Easy, brother. Easy. You will not pay for Cruz's crimes tonight. On three, this bad boy is coming out. One…" Rafi doesn't finish the count, but rips the blade from Santos' thigh, spilling more blood and fresh guilt onto the carpet.

Santos shudders against Rafi, who pulls him in for a hug.

I should be hugging him. Both of them. They're my brothers now, and I'm treating them like…

I feel a tug I wish wasn't there. Feelings are toxic, but it's what our family demands.

Santos releases Rafi and grabs the ripped bedsheet, pulling it down and tearing off strips with trembling fingers. He winds the strip around his thigh while Rafi goes on a steady stream of asking how he can help, which is only broken up by peppered-in sentences where he puts me in my proper place.

Santos ties off his leg and crawls to Adelita without looking up at me once. He doesn't appear angry, nor does he question me. He's a good soldier who wouldn't dare turn on his commander, which somehow makes this whole thing worse.

Santos scoops Adelita up off the floor, but I'm not sure he has the fortitude to lift her just yet. Instead he tucks his body into the corner and cradles her limp form across his lap. His expression is tender when he drinks in the sight of her sweaty face.

Santos has never held a woman before, but somehow his arms know what to do.

With the way he brushes a stray curl from Adelita's forehead, I know I've gone too far.

7

SOMEONE TO LEAN ON

RAFAEL

"Not hungry?" I ask our second quiet member of the group. With Santos not able to speak, Adelita refusing to talk, and Cruz and I giving each other the silent treatment, it's just about the most boring morning I've ever endured. It almost sucks the fun out of eating my frosted, untoasted breakfast pastry.

Almost.

Adelita gives me a small shake of her head, but there's no malice in it. She clings to the corner, still wearing that bloodied, torn pink silk blouse.

"Cruz bought you new clothes. You sure you don't want to try them on? You might look less like you've been recently murdered if you're not wearing blood-stained clothes."

She eyes the bag warily and shakes her head again. She looks like death warmed over. Filthy clothes aside, she's lost a lot of blood. Her raven hair has half-fallen out of its bun, surrounding her sallow complexion with waves that make her look like a rock star on her last leg. I doubt she slept a wink beyond when she lost consciousness for those brief minutes. She needs food and a shower, and I'm fairly certain she won't let any of us help her with either.

Cruz doesn't do remorse gracefully; it only makes him surlier. He scowls at her as he stands in their motel room, though I'm not sure why. "You need to change before we go. You'll only draw attention to yourself, looking like that."

It's been all night and morning she's been silent, but at this, she turns to Santos with a mournful expression. "I can't!" she whispers. "I can't get my blouse off without moving my shoulder. I'm not trying to be difficult; I just don't know how to do it without making everything worse."

I swallow my sleezy comment about me being able to help her out of her clothes. I'm guessing being hit on is the last thing she needs right about now.

Compassion floods Santos' features. It's clear to me why she finally chose him to confess a problem to. His shoulders lean in and he holds up a hand with a solemn expression, communicating that he can take care of that problem.

She trusts Santos enough to let him help her to her feet. It's kind of sweet to watch her lean on him. I've never seen Santos near a woman who wasn't Cruz's sister. And Eva doesn't lean on anyone—least of all one of us, her annoying brothers. The care Santos takes with her as he leads her into the bathroom astounds me. He even grabs her change of clothes and her purse that we snagged from the parking lot encounter.

I know he didn't learn that from Cruz or from me, yet it's clear Santos is exactly the sort of understanding soul Adelita needs right now.

"You're an ass," I say to Cruz the second the bathroom door closes them off from us. It's not my best insult, nor is it the greatest way to start out a dialogue, but Cruz gets what he gets at this point. *"Tonto del culo."*

He shrugs and plops atop Santos' mattress, as if he doesn't

care about any of it. But I know he does, because I saw the look on his face when Santos stabbed himself. Plus, the sky hasn't cleared of its dark clouds all morning. That's the biggest tell of all. He feels guilt; he just doesn't know what to do with it.

Santos is our responsibility. When he does stuff like this —hurts himself when he doesn't understand the world—it's our fault. We didn't educate him enough. For how reformed we brag he is to the tribe, seeing a knife jutting out of his thigh because he doesn't know how to question Cruz guts me every time.

"What's the plan for today, oh fearless leader?"

Cruz doesn't look at me. "Get her back to the tribe. Let Tio Bruno deal with her. He can get info out of her better than me."

I fight the urge to leap onto the mattress he's sitting atop and strangle him. Though, as he's my best friend, my adoptive brother and my superior, I only visualize the assault in the same way one dreams about Christmas presents.

"You'll do no such thing. Tio Bruno's even worse than you are. You're trying to break the puzzle instead of solving it. Not everything can be mastered with brute force. Some situations need finesse."

"What are you suggesting? Can you honestly picture her leaning on me the way she was with Santos just now?"

I quirk my eyebrow at Cruz's strange observation. I always assume he's obtuse about relational stuff, but even he noticed trust starting to bloom.

Just not in his direction.

"Is that what you want? For Adelita to lean on you? Because tearing open her stiches is a funny way to show it."

"Shut up. I don't want anything like that."

I glance up at the ceiling, putting on as much ease as I can fake. "Well, your way landed you here, where she's afraid to go near the bag of clothes you bought her. Santos' way gets him exactly where you wish you were—helping Adelita out of her clothes."

Cruz's chin whips toward me, his nostrils flaring. My eyebrow quirks, awaiting his comeback, but his phone interrupts us.

He answers the call with a succinct, "What? No, sir." A few beats of pause, and then monosyllabic responses come before he hangs up. His eyes dart to mine. "Tio Bruno wants us to check out the curse tree in Buckley. Four members of the Kalku were spotted there just now. We should go."

"We will. Go load up the car so Adelita can shower without worrying you're going to break in there and hurt her again." I could say it with a sneer, but I don't. The truth doesn't need extra bitterness added to it.

Cruz stands and pounds his fist to the bathroom door. "Hurry it up in there, Santos. Tio Bruno called. We need to go check out one of the curse trees."

I snigger when there's no response from the other side.

Cruz flips me his middle finger before stomping out to load up the car.

Yes, we're off to a great start.

8

SCARRED SWEETNESS
ADELITA

My breath comes in heavy pants. I'm exhausted, for one. I'm hungry and my whole body feels sluggish. On top of that, Santos pulls out a serrated blade that looks too menacing to be near me. If not for the calm caution in his eyes, I would run out of here screaming, for sure.

"But what about your thigh?" I question, unable to understand why he's bent on helping me when it's clear he's in pain from his self-inflicted wound.

He manages a wan smile that doesn't touch his eyes. He is in pain, but he's more concerned about my welfare.

He mimes cutting my shirt to warn me that's the only way it can come off without hurting my shoulder more. Before I can get anxious, he covers his eyes in a silent promise he won't look.

"Well, you can't close your eyes when you've got a knife to my collar!"

He draws a chuckle from me when he solves the problem by closing one eye, as if that would fix it all.

I can't hide my smile. "Thank you. That's much better."

He waits for my consent before clearing the foot of a gap between us in the tight space.

He cuts a notch at the collar of the pink silk and then steps so close, our stomachs are almost touching. He sets the knife on the sink and makes a show of closing his eyes.

Santos presses his chin to my forehead, which is just about the only way I want a man to touch me right now. Even as he rips my blouse open from top to bottom, all I can think is that his skin is the only warm thing in my universe.

Though the tearing of my blouse doesn't hurt, I gasp all the same. He keeps his chin on my hairline, and I realize he's doing that to assure me he's not looking. I'm relieved to the point of nearly getting emotional, but I limit my outpouring of gratitude to a simple "thank you."

Cruz barks something from the other side of the door, but I don't pay attention. I've been cold all night, but Santos' chin is the first spot of heat I've been able to hold on to. I'm tired, and he feels like pure rest.

When Santos pops open the button on my slacks, I decide I can figure out the rest on my own. "I can do that part. Thanks for not making this more humiliating than it has to be."

He keeps his chin on my forehead while he cuts my sling off. The whole thing is bizarrely comforting, despite all I've been through in less than twenty-four hours.

I can't remember the last time a man was so careful with me.

Come to think of it, I can't remember the last time I was close enough to smell my favorite spot on a man—the crook of his neck. Though I don't have my nose buried where it wants to be, it's close enough to give me that hit of euphoria I try not to crave.

Smelling boys' necks won't get you closer to graduation.

Smelling boys' necks won't help your patients.

Still, the scent of Santos teases me in my weakened state. He smells like aftershave and fresh plants that are just on the verge of blooming.

When Santos' fingers tap on the bra strap that's far too taut on my right shoulder, a blush warms my cheeks. My left bra strap was cut off yesterday so Santos could stitch me up. The whole contraption is barely useable. Still, as much as Santos has been decent through this whole ordeal, I don't want my imagination to run away with me, which is exactly what will happen if he unhooks my bra. He's five inches taller than me, so I make it a point not to lift my chin at all. If I look into his eyes from this close, it'll be bad. The whole thing will be too much. He's being kind, and I'm acting like a horny teenager on the verge of panting.

"No, thanks," I reply to his unspoken request. I'll get the remnants of my bra off myself. Somehow. "I've got it from here."

Santos lowers his chin just enough to let his full lips brush over my forehead. It's not a kiss, but it's intimate.

Or maybe it's not intimate at all, and I'm so out of practice being near a man that I'm imagining a love connection smack in the middle of a medical moment.

I've never had a man kiss me there before, but for some reason, just the brush of his lips is the perfect thing to keep me from toppling over the edge of this-is-all-too-much. There's a sweetness to his eyes that's not flirty but sincere. The scarring on his face is ghastly, yet his gentleness still shines through the lines that should never have been drawn into his skin.

Santos keeps his eyes from me as he starts up the water, and then does something so sweet, I can barely stand it. With his eyes closed, he kneels down and removes my socks. My filthy, sweaty socks.

It's precious, and I feel too war-torn to be in the same room as such sweetness.

"You don't have to do that. You're limping still. You shouldn't be kneeling."

He picks up his chin but looks to the side with a shrug, and dang, if he doesn't have the longest, blackest eyelashes I've ever seen.

I should tell him about my encounter with Santiago, but I can't seem to wrap my mind around how crazy it all sounds. A man pulled me from the burning bus, blessed me and then vanished? I never told anyone about it. I've always kept that wild event to myself.

I convinced myself it was a hallucination born of trauma, which according to all my years of study, is on the edge of normal, given the situation. I guess I never thought it would all feel so very real.

And I never imagined I would stumble upon his twin brother, slamming me in the face with the reality that something irreconcilable was begging me to solve it.

My rescuer was real. And unfortunately, he's dead now.

When Santos stands, he angles his hips not to bump into anything as he slides gracefully from the room, shutting me in the small space while my knees quake.

Santiago wore sandals and cutoffs when he pulled me from the wreckage. Santos is a sight in ripped jeans and a black t-shirt, the mirror image of his brother, exact in poise and that calm demeanor. It's that series of scars marking up Santos' face that makes the two distinct. With his chin-length hair in his face and left cheek scarred, I didn't see the shocking similarity at first.

I keep my shower as quick as I can, for fear of some catastrophe happening where I might possibly be pulled naked from the shower.

I don't want to look at my stitches in the mirror when I

emerge, clean but still shaken. I don't want to *have* stitches. I'm grateful for the fog that covers over the glass so I can't clearly see myself and the mess that I am. Being clean is a nice luxury, though, so I decide to be grateful for at least that.

My fingers are clumsy and weak as I try to tug my new jeans on one-handed. They're not too bad a fit, and slide over my curvy hips without too much struggle. It's the black t-shirt that gives me problems. I can't lift my left arm to thread it through after I manage to work the thing over my head.

I decide to take a break from the frustration and sit on the toilet lid. I pull out my phone from my purse, texting Tomás that I won't be in to work for the rest of the week.

When I can't struggle with my shirt anymore, I finally make the chagrinned call to Santos through the door. "Santos? Are you there?"

"Just me, *linda.* Santos is showering in my room. What do you need?"

"Nothing. I'll figure it out."

"I'm coming in."

I hold tight to the handle in a panic. "No! I'm okay. It's just this shirt. I can't get it on without moving my shoulder, which I really can't do. I'm afraid I'm going to rip open my stitches."

Rafael's voice loses a bit of its play. "Fine. Then I'm coming in with my eyes closed. It's either that, or you get in the car topless. I'm not opposed to that option but it might be more attention than we're hoping to attract."

I grab the damp towel and cover my breasts, mortified that this is how my morning is going. I need to lie down; my head feels muddled and my limbs are sluggish.

I lower my chin as I sit back down atop the toilet lid. "Okay, fine. This is just the worst."

Rafael grins. "Is it really? Because I'm having a great day all of a sudden."

He's just goofy enough to make me groan at his awful humor. For some reason, him trying to get under my skin sets loose my personality, which I've been trying to keep away from them.

His stupid jokes remind me to give myself permission to exhale every now and then. Not every moment is harrowing. Not every encounter needs an exhausting amount of scrutiny.

Rafael comes in with his eyes closed, but then harrumphs and opens them. "Well, what's the point if you're going to be all covered up?"

"You were peeking!" I accuse with an indignant huff.

"At your scandalous towel? Sure, I guess I was. Come on, let me help you before Cruz gets in here. I'm guessing you don't want assistance from our fearless leader?"

That's the bucket of cold water over my head, for sure. No way do I want Cruz to see me like this. "I can't get it… And this part is just…"

"I can help. Hold still. Mind if I stretch out the shirt a little?"

"Fine by me."

He yanks at the collar that's dangling around my neck like it's a dog's play toy, pulling it until the fabric creaks. "That's better. Okay, it still might hurt, but I'll make sure nothing tears your stitches."

I bite down on my lower lip and nod, readying myself for yet more pain.

Rafael is gentle in his fluid movements, stretching the shirt to its limits so he can thread my arm through. It hurts, and for a second, I'm certain the stitches have ripped open again, but when it's all said and done, the pain was the worst of it, and my wound remains untorn.

"Thank you. Oh, that's much better to not be in bloody, filthy clothes."

He tips his chin to me. "You sure you don't need my help getting *out* of your shirt? I'm much better at that end of things. Dressing a woman is counterintuitive."

I mime a laugh and actually find myself grinning, which I'll admit, I didn't think possible today. "Thanks for making a joke. This is all a bit much for me."

He sits down on the edge of the tub so he can level with me. He stares into my eyes with a seriousness that is so strange to see, I can't look away. "Look, I know Cruz went about everything the wrong way. He doesn't think sometimes. He's military, and little else."

My mouth tightens. "If this is the part where you stick up for him, you can save it."

"It's not. He was wrong, and I won't defend him. He'd only be angry at me if I did. I just wanted to tell you that whatever secret it is that you're holding on to, we can't help you if we don't have all the facts. And if the Kalku are after you, then like it or not, you'll need our help."

I mull over his words before offering up a succinct nod. "I'll take that into consideration."

Rafael lets out a long sigh. "Well, it looks like I have no other choice. If Cruz couldn't torture the information out of you, it's time to send in the closer."

He stands and turns his backside to me, and I truly have no idea what to expect.

Then he starts up a slow shimmy, shaking his butt in my face just to make me laugh. "What? I'm to seduce the truth from you. Or would you prefer some of this action instead?" He turns at the sound of my giggles spilling out all over the tiled floor and jiggles his shoulders as if he'd very much like to shake his invisible boobs in my face. "This isn't working, I see. Time to unload the fart blaster."

"I confess! I confess!" I laugh, the back of my hand swooning across my forehead. "My secret is that I'm allergic to terrible dancing and toxic farts. Stop it now, or I'll break out in hives!"

He stops undulating and stands straight, his mouth pouting with affront. "'Terrible dancing'? You're a cruel lover, Adelita. Beautiful but cruel."

He fake cries loudly as I shove him out the bathroom door. Then he pops right back in with a toothbrush and toothpaste, which are just about the best things he could possibly show me. "How much do you love me now? A travel toothbrush pretty much means you're in with the cool kids."

"Lucky me." Though, I'm so grateful, I could cry. Brushing my teeth makes me feel that much more human.

Everything I do is slower, and done while fighting through brain fog and clumsy fingers, but I manage to clean myself up enough to stumble out into the main room and sit on the bed.

Cruz comes in, refusing to look at me while he picks up my purse. "Car," is all he says to me by way of an invitation.

I don't want to go anywhere with him, but the puzzle is too intriguing now. I truly have no idea who the Kalku are or what their end game is in attacking me.

Cruz is a bastard, for sure, but he has answers, so I follow him out of the motel and into the unknown.

9

SILENT ROAD TRIP
CRUZ

'm not the type to need senseless chatter while I drive. I should be grateful for the quiet, but the absence of Rafi's usual incessant ramblings sets my teeth on edge. This woman is throwing off our dynamic with her silence.

Santos is in the backseat beside her. He's been a wolf for most of the morning, leaning into her touch each time she smooths her hand over his fur.

I can't decide why I hate this, but I do. I've never seen Santos show interest in a woman before. It's only been two-and-a-half years since he's been introduced to silverware and shampoo.

Eva fawned all over Santos while she educated him on proper society. I thought he would fall for my sister, for sure. All the soldiers stand taller when she walks into the barracks. Yet Santos took no romantic interest in her, the daughter of the chief. It's just as well, since Dad adopted him a month after he was liberated from the Kalku.

But this woman, the daughter of no one, he can't be parted from. I don't get it.

It's cloudy. The weather is always gloomy when I'm agitated, but as I can see sun in the distance, the overcast atmosphere all around us is that much more irksome. Dad would tell me to meditate. To try and let some things go so my moods don't interfere with nature this much.

I'm positive the quiet will break Rafi before me.

Or maybe not.

At hour five, I finally splinter the silence. "Who wants what for lunch? I need to refuel and stretch my legs."

Rafi looks at me like I'm crazy. "You seriously think stopping is a good idea? Our tail is still two cars behind us."

I swerve slightly with the shock and adjust my rearview mirror to see what Rafi's talking about.

Sure enough, the camo-dressed members of the Kalku foot soldiers are a couple cars behind us. I swear under my breath. "How long have they been following us?"

Rafi turns to frown at me. "Three hours. You really didn't notice? I thought you were playing it safe and leading them toward the tribe so we have more backup."

I glower at him in lieu of an answer, which brings us back to that uncomfortable silence.

I didn't notice.

I didn't see something that was obvious for three whole hours.

I don't know what my problem is, but it stops now.

I pull off the freeway and keep a steady pace. I have no intention of relying on the tribe for help fighting off this handful of Kalku. There are children in the tribe.

Plus, Tio Bruno would look down on me if I brought the intruders onto our land instead of handling them myself. If the Kalku want to follow us, I'm going to find out why. I'm also going to find out how they tracked us down in the first place. I can't have this hanging over our heads. They must have found a way to track Adelita.

"Give me your phone, Adelita."

She doesn't do as I say, which bothers me to no end. Instead she digs into her purse and hands her device to Santos, placing it in his maw. It's a blatant display, an outright defiance to make a point that she doesn't trust me.

Right now there are bigger fish to fry than her petulance.

Santos has been a wolf all morning, keeping to his silence. While I know he heals faster in his wolf form, his choice feels like a purposeful silence because I hurt Adelita.

"Rafi, check her phone for a tracker. I may have missed it. I pulled out the one, but if there's a second, I didn't see it."

"Tracker?" she echoes, her small voice finally making an appearance. "The Kalku put a tracker on my phone?"

Santos deposits the device in Rafi's palm, who pries off the back to examine the circuitry.

"The one I took out I smashed far from the motel, but still they found you."

Adelita's arm is angled, so I'm fairly certain she's got her hand in her lap, finally taking a break from petting Santos. "Why do you assume it's me? Couldn't the Kalku be keeping tabs on *you*? I mean, you were also at the clinic."

Finally she speaks to me, and all it does is remind me how little she knows about the world that's been bubbling beneath the surface of her suburban life.

I grip the steering wheel while Rafi thumbs through her apps. "Only Kalku with a death wish would target me. I've killed more of them than anyone."

"Seems like you'd be the perfect person to target."

"Nice try."

She scoffs. "Excuse me?"

"I know what you're trying to do. You're diverting the attention from yourself so we don't pry into why the Kalku want you. You think I don't know you know exactly why they're after you?"

She shifts in her seat, and for the life of me, I cannot understand why she's not wearing a bra. I didn't mean to get her a black t-shirt a size too small, but with each uneven patch on the road, her breasts bounce like they're trying to distract me.

Santos' head rests on her thigh like she's his owner or something. His nose lifts so he can lick the underside of her chin.

She smiles only for him this morning, and runs her fingers over his fur. Does she understand that he's kissing her? His neck brushes against hers and I struggle not to snap.

Though what I could say, I have no idea.

It's her mouth that breaks me out of that train of thought, thank goodness. "How would I possibly know something like that? I'm a therapist. Nothing more exciting than that. I didn't even know those people existed until yesterday."

My jaw ticks. "You think I don't know when I'm being lied to?"

Rafi casts me a look of sheer exasperation at the sharpness of my tone. "Wouldn't hurt to check the car for trackers once we deal with our tail."

Unbelievable. The trust in my ability to lead is crumbling left and right all because Adelita can't seem to grasp that I'm the one who rescued her. I'm the one in charge. I'm the one who was at the right place at the right time to intervene when the Kalku attacked her.

Rafi hisses as he taps on her phone. "What's the plan, Cruz? They're closing in on us."

My eyes flicker back to the mirror, which is where they should've been. My stomach sinks when I notice it's not just one car but now two that aren't playing coy any longer. One's on our right, with his front bumper a few feet behind mine, and the other's readying to close in on the left.

"Buckle up," I warn.

Santos turns back into his man form and holds up his finger to pause my attack on the cars. He unbuckles Adelita and slides her to the middle seat, fastening her in place again before giving me a nod. He's got one hand on the back of my seat and the other gripping Adelita's headrest.

"What's happening?" Adelita frets. "Santos, what are you doing?"

I know what he's doing; I only wish I knew if him using his body as a shield for her will be worth it.

The moment Adelita's belt is in place, I swerve into the left lane, clipping the offending car enough to spin it off its course.

Adelita's scream goes straight to my spine, tightening everything inside of me. We know not to tense when we hit another car, but I forget too many things as I correct our trajectory.

When the driver on my right veers too near Rafi, my blood boils. Come after Adelita, sure, but Rafi has been by my side since we were young.

Rafi turns on his dragon characteristics, since those are more difficult to penetrate.

I jerk the car perhaps a little too hard, smashing them clear off the road and into the ditch. If they can get their car out of there, it'll be a miracle.

My car's fine, and theirs is dented like tin foil. How it should be. Thank you, SUVs. Built for soccer moms and defenders of tribes.

I blow out a breath in a long stream before Rafi speaks. "It's her they're after. Found spyware on her phone. Intercepted the data stream and sent it to my phone instead. We'll be able to hear everything they've recorded and how long they've been listening in."

"What?" Adelita croaks. Her eyes are wide with betrayal, as if she can't believe someone would dare violate her precious privacy. "Why are they listening to my phone calls?"

"You'd know better than us."

She leans forward, so near Santos, she could practically be in his arms. "Does this look like a woman in the know?"

I grip the steering wheel, my teeth on edge as the car I clipped finally rights itself and peels after us. "I'm guessing it's got something to do with you knowing Santiago."

She clams up again, but I can see she's finally starting to understand that there's a much bigger world than she realized. Her secrets will do her no good if she's captured.

I try to keep my hands steady on the wheel, but when the rear windshield blows out from the force of a brick through the glass, her scream tears a new hole through my resolve.

I jerk the car to the side of the road, throw it into park and launch myself out. Rafi's tight on my heels, running with me toward the car that's driving with a wobbly wheel. If they want her, they'll have to go through us.

Only they don't go through us. I swear in a sharp burst as they veer around us and head straight for my car.

Rafi cries out as we turn directions and bolt for Santos and Adelita, who are still in the vehicle.

My heart leaps up in my throat, choking me with all the ways I would never recover if anything ever happened to Santos. I see Santos' life flash before my eyes, but just before they ram the back of my car, a flash of their brake lights give me hope. They still bump my car, but not enough to kill on impact.

They don't want to kill her, I realize. *They want to take her.*

They fling open their doors, knives drawn as they dart out. Two men in the back run at Rafi and me, no doubt to slow us down. The other two go for my car, throwing open the backdoor and yelling at Santos and Adelita to come out now.

They know her name. They knew where we'd be. The Kalku collect women of value to their dark purposes.

No matter what Adelita says, it's undeniable that she's valuable to the Kalku.

10

THE DEATH OF US

CRUZ

Stupid, stupid Kalku. They trained Santos in their own manner of fighting, but when I freed him, I combined his upbringing with that of our soldiers.

They call him Santos the Savage, which is a cruel, yet well-earned nickname in the tribe.

Santos launches himself out of the backseat like a cannon, ignoring the threat of the knives while he wrestles and bites and rips at the two men in camo.

There's no rain, but lightning strikes in the distance, announcing to the world that I'm angry.

"Don't let them take Santos!" Rafi shouts as three men from the ditched car pound the pavement behind us. "I've got these guys. You help Santos!" He turns on his heel and charges in the opposite direction after disposing of his attacker. Rafi works with me as if he's part of my brain.

My assailant is easy to gut. I can tell he's scared of me before we even collide. Smart guy.

When Santos stabs the first man and is knocked in the head by the second, it's clear they're not after him alone. I can't decide if that should fill me with relief, or if knowing they're after Adelita is worse. They've long-since given up on stealing Santos back.

I intercept one of the three men from the second car, but the other two breeze past me towards Santos.

Santos is dazed, but I can tell he's only getting started. One of him on three of them isn't nearly a fair fight. They shouldn't have trained Santos so well. He's utterly vicious in hand-to-hand combat.

I'm nearly to them when my stomach drops at the shock of black hair emerging from the vehicle. "Stay in the car!" I shout to Adelita as thunder cracks overhead.

Santos is being kicked from behind while he chokes out the second Kalku, but his eyes go wide to warn Adelita not to involve herself. He can handle this, even with a blow to the head.

The third assailant is distracted by an attack from Rafi, thank the clouds. Cars are careening by, and it's all any of us can do not to get caught in the morning rush.

When Adelita pays me no mind, I can't get to them fast enough. "Get back in the car!" I shout.

But she doesn't listen, which is no great surprise. Instead, she limps around the front end and grips the guy who's kicking Santos in the spine. She yanks him by the belt and jerks him back.

I'm not sure what I'm seeing. How can he not shake her grip?

"Don't touch him!" she yells like a little girl on the playground defending her friend from a bully.

My mouth falls open when the dainty mouse launches the Kalku with one hand straight into his car's dented frame. The entire structure groans with force that just can't be possible.

I trip and nearly fall forward at the sight. My mind can't make sense of it. When his body slumps to the ground, I blanch at the man's caved-in skull. Like bad paper mâché, the top of his head is now flattened down to his nose. "What the..."

Santos is equally stunned, and loses his grip on the Kalku he's trying to choke out. The camo-clad idiot is granted a few more life-sustaining breaths, which Adelita deems is one too many.

With her only functioning arm, she grips the man's bicep and rips him from Santos. She whips his body against the side of his own car over and over until he's a limp, broken noodle that slumps when she finally lets go.

She's got tears in her eyes, but that doesn't stop her from running away from the wreckage toward Rafi. I should follow and offer backup, but I'm too stunned for movement.

I watch with a mixture of amazement and horror as she intervenes in a similar fashion for Rafi. Her fist knocks Rafi's full-grown assailant at least fifteen feet back. Her assault snaps his head to the side so powerfully, I'm certain he must be concussed.

When he somehow finds the fortitude to stand, she grabs his collar, ignoring his pleas for mercy.

A member of the Kalku actually begging for mercy. Never thought I'd see the day. The whole thing is so strange that I find myself staring uselessly at the scene, unsure of anything at this point.

With her left arm still in its sling, Adelita lifts the last of the Kalku off his feet and launches his body farther than I would have guessed possible. My eyes follow until a sickening thud can be heard over the rush of cars as the man splats on the concrete.

She's breathing hard while Rafi swears with wide eyes, his bloodied, olive-scaled fingers gripping his hair. "What was that? How did you..."

She won't look at us. When she glances at her victims, she

winces at the sight of the blood, like she can't believe she's capable of such violence.

The woman took down three Kalku with one hand and no weapons. I mean, I've done that before, but never so brutally, and not without walking away looking like I'd taken the business end of a bad beating myself.

When her wet, guilty eyes meet mine, I can see her sifting through too many options that might try to explain this away.

Maldito, she's cute.

Adelita bleats a pitiful, "I... I didn't do it!"

The snigger that escapes my lips must sound sociopathic, but I can't help it.

She turns to run from me, but stops at Rafi's raised arms. He's not signaling a surrender, but offering the shaken woman a hug.

I've never seen a woman touch Rafi when he was part-dragon like this. Most run the other way.

Adelita falls into his green arms with a sob. "I didn't mean to! They were going to hurt Santos! They were hurting *you!*"

It's finally clear to me why the Kalku have tracked her down. They know she's got superhuman strength.

I have no idea how Rafi finds the presence of mind to keep his voice controlled with a calm lightness. "It's alright, *linda*. You don't have to think about that right now. I didn't see a thing. All I know is some sexy gust of wind did me a solid and took care of the guys who outnumbered us. Man, if only I could thank that wind."

Only Rafi can make a person laugh when they're mid-crisis. His smile at her chuckle tells me somehow things will be alright. I don't know how, but Rafi's ease often gives me that hope. I've never told him how much I rely on that optimism to get us through.

He tucks a stray curl behind her ear, and something in my chest tightens. "Thank you, *viento*," he says to her.

She nods into his shoulder while she sniffles, her free arm reaching up to thumb at his collar to cling to him that much more.

I don't understand her tears. Or maybe it's not that I don't understand them, but rather that I don't understand how she's so free with them. Crying is a weakness. That's a simple fact. Yet she just did the impossible, all while broadcasting raw emotion.

I'm fascinated by each tear, while equally disgusted.

Santos limps toward them and Rafi smiles at him, motioning him forward. He hands Adelita off after placing a kiss to her unmarked shoulder. It's a small blessing of sweetness, but it flips my stomach.

When she folds easily into Santos' arms, my throat goes dry.

She may have saved us this time, but when my chest tightens at the moisture sparkling on the apple of her cheek, I am certain this woman is going to be the death of us.

11

MILKSHAKES AND MUSCLE
SANTOS

*I*t doesn't take long for Cruz to lose his temper with Adelita's tight lips. It's not just overcast outside now, but the clouds have turned thunderous with his anger. He knows much about many things, but he understands zero about this woman.

So I study her. The small motions of her fingers as she fiddles with the hem of her black t-shirt. The way she keeps her head down, even though our windows are tinted. She's shaken by the deeds of her own hands, which tells me she hasn't often tapped into this enhancement.

I want to ask her a million questions, but none of them matter unless she's willing to answer. Judging by the way she's hugging the car door as Cruz barrels down the highway, it will be a long time before she's willing to open up.

"Are you trying to drive me crazy? We all saw you murder them. We know you're stronger than most people because we just saw it! What possible reason could you have for keeping quiet when we have questions?"

But she keeps herself locked tight, staring out the window, her chin downward.

"We've got bigger problems," Rafi informs us, finally looking up from his phone. "Sorry, *viento*. This has to be done."

Rafi rolls down his window and chucks her phone on to the side of the road, drawing a scandalized gasp from her lips.

A look of intrigue crosses his features as he turns in his seat toward her, his eyebrows dancing with mischief. "Would you like to yell at me?"

Adelita falls for the bait, finally speaking.

"Why did you do that? I need my phone."

"Actually, your phone is the thing that's directing the Kalku right to you. The text you sent this morning gave them all they needed to find you."

"What?" Cruz thunders, and a crack echoes in the skies in the distance to match his temper. "In what world do you imagine I gave you permission to use your phone?"

I groan internally, wishing Cruz would learn how to listen instead of bark out commands. She was just crying, and doesn't need to be yelled at.

True to expectation, she clams up and hugs the door again. I like her closer than this, and Cruz is purposefully putting her on edge. Her entire being is pure warmth, and I feel cold without her near me.

"I asked you a question, Adelita."

Her lips tighten. "I thought it was clear that I'm ignoring all asinine commands today."

"Look at Rafi's knuckles. They're scraped up because he was fighting off Kalku who wouldn't have known where we were if you hadn't tipped them off. You might think *you're* angry, but *I'm* furious! And sure, my car can withstand a lot, but I'm going to need a realignment now, for sure, at the very least."

A flicker of agony crosses her big, blue eyes when she glances up to the front to gape at Rafael's hands.

Rafi shoots Cruz a wry look as if to say his injury is obviously nothing.

He's right; Cruz is making a big deal of it to guilt Adelita into seeing the bigger picture.

"And how many times in your life have you been knocked in the head? Santos could've gotten himself a concussion. Not to mention the blows to his back he probably wasn't hoping for when he woke up this morning."

I sigh in frustration at Cruz, catching his eye in the rearview mirror. It's clear that I'm fine. I'm barely sore from the swift kicks. I don't want Cruz implying that I can't handle myself. My attacker only got so many licks in because I was occupied with the other guy.

Cruz digs the knife in deeper, as is his way. "You want to tell me who you were texting?"

"What does that matter?"

"Well, they could be in league with the Kalku."

Adelita shuts her mouth but Rafi answers. "She texted a man named Tomás."

She lowers her chin. "He needs to know to cancel my caseload for the week."

She didn't call a friend or her family. She called her job to make sure they weren't left high and dry. It's responsible, yes, but sad.

Rafael seems to be on my same train of thought. "You called work and not a friend? No relatives will miss you when you're gone?"

"I'm sure I won't be gone long." She speaks with feigned confidence, avoiding his question. As she says the words, I know she's pushing more hope behind them than she believes. She evades the things she doesn't want to talk about more artfully than I was taught to dodge blows.

Rafael claps Cruz on the shoulder. "That's alright, *viento*. Cruz doesn't have any friends either, besides us. We'll be your friends."

She sniggers at Cruz's bristling as he shakes off Rafi's hand. "Thank you."

When her stomach growls, I lean forward, drawing Cruz's eye. I sign that it's time to stop for something to eat, and he nods once. "Give me twenty more miles, just to be safe. I want to put some distance between us and the scene of the crime, just in case they're still trying to find us."

It's the longest twenty miles of my life because her stomach growls five times. I don't know why Cruz doesn't stop. He must not hear it, because every time I do, it's all I can do to keep myself from insisting we pull over now. Her face is impassive as she stares out the window, her free arm banded around her midsection to muffle the sound.

When we arrive at a diner called Egg in the Basket, I'm quick to exit, rounding the car to help her out.

It's clear she doesn't need assistance, but she takes my hand all the same.

I love that. I want to be helpful. It's addictive to be near her. Every time she allows it, I savor the trust I'm not often granted.

When Adelita stands, I don't let go of her hand right away, but sandwich it between mine so I can indulge in her warmth a little while longer.

The best part about it is that she lets me hold on to her hand. She doesn't recoil from my touch. No doubt she would if she knew more about me or my upbringing.

For now, I let myself believe it would be no different if she knew every detail of the wickedness where I was raised.

I let go when I catch Cruz's careful study of me. He doesn't like Adelita, and *really* doesn't like it when my focus is divided. I step back so I can guard her from behind, though what I can save her from that she can't do herself is beyond me. I've never seen anyone with that kind of strength, and I've witnessed my fair share of massacres.

The diner is dirtier than Cruz prefers, but he's always been more particular about that kind of thing.

Rafi doesn't waste time flagging down the waitress. She comes around to take our drink requests, and Cruz places meal orders for the three of us right away. Water for me, coffee for him, and one of every flavor of milkshake for Rafael. Cruz always orders for everyone. Two burgers apiece for the three of us.

"What do you want, *viento*?"

Adelita thumbs at the menu. "Just some coffee would be good."

I frown at her and tap the corner of the menu to indicate she should eat something.

"I'm too nervous to eat," she admits right as her stomach rumbles.

I sign to her that she needs iron after losing so much blood yesterday. Rafael interprets for me.

Before she can put up a rebuttal, Rafael orders her a full breakfast, going over her head. When she frowns at him, he shrugs off the guilt as only he can do. "What? Can't have you fainting again. Doctor's orders." He inclines his head to me.

She tucks the menu behind the sugar caddy and exhales in a long string of exposed nerves. "Can we just get this over with? Whatever the interrogation's going to be, just do it. I don't want to barf up everything in my stomach if it's going to be brutal."

Her eyes flick furtively to Cruz and then tear away, like a skittish animal afraid of a free meal. I don't like the look of fear on her, least of all when it's directed at Cruz, to whom I owe my life. I want to confidently assure her that of course

Cruz won't resort to hurting her again, but the fact that "again" has to be included undercuts my argument.

Rafael's hand bats away her concern, but his jaw ticks with anger over what Cruz did this morning, ripping open her stitches. "Aw, you don't have to worry about that. We know your big secret. Maybe Cruz will want more details about how you got this way, but I'm sure that's nothing to worry about. Right, big guy?"

Rafi claps Cruz on the shoulder in a manner that looks amiable enough, but really it's a silent warning. The line was crossed once, but Rafi won't tolerate it again.

The knot in my chest slowly loosens that we might not have to go through that twice. Rafi will stand up to Cruz in ways I would never dare. I owe Cruz too much to cross or question him.

I wish I could stand up to Cruz like that, but the truth of the matter is, I don't know the world as well as he does. He's lived in the free air his whole life, and comparatively speaking, I'm only two years familiar with freedom. I still don't have a driver's license. So I trust that Cruz knows best. Besides, I don't have it in me to go against him. He freed me from the Kalku; I owe him my life. I don't want to think of what might happen if I displease him. He might cast me out of the tribe. I know I'm only allowed into the city because he vouched for me. I have a legal father now, a mother, siblings and a home that isn't a cave.

Of course, even though the chief adopted me, that doesn't stop the rest of the village from looking at me as if I'm a rabid animal, ready to pounce on their young and tear the whole village apart.

Cruz treats me like a man and took the time to rehabilitate me. He believed there was goodness in me. Because of that, I have to believe that everything he does must have some shred of goodness to it.

But that doesn't erase the sound of Adelita's screams when he hurt her on purpose. My fist tightens on my fork at the memory.

Cruz doesn't acknowledge Rafi's edict that he won't use force to interrogate her again, but he doesn't contradict it either. I guess that's the best we'll get. "How long?" Cruz says to her.

She shakes her head, and beneath the table, I feel her foot nervously tapping out a skittish rhythm.

The sound is going to drive Cruz to insanity.

"You first. You all talk about a tribe and magic and whatnot. Is that what you are? A warlock?"

To his credit, Cruz doesn't scoff. He doesn't answer, either. He's stalwart that his words will be heeded. He asked her a question first, so even though what we are is no big secret, he holds on to it as a bargaining chip. "How long have you been able to throw grown men around and crack their skulls one-handed?"

She lowers her chin. The clinking of silverware and drone of conversations all around us nearly drown out her meek reply. "Forever. But I mean, I've never m-murdered anyone before this."

"Who else knows?"

The napkin in front of her finds its way to her hand so she can tear off small bits of it and line up the pieces in a row. It's the strangest nervous tick, but it keeps her talking, so I guess it helps her. "I think Tomás was passed out when I intervened at the clinic when the Kalku jumped him, but it's possible he saw more than I wanted him to. So the only people who for sure know my secret are the three of you."

"No family? No friends?" Cruz asks.

He may need the verbal clarification but I don't. All I need is to look at Rafael. If he trusts her answer, that's enough for me. Rafi can spot a lie a mile away, no doubt because he's told so many. He's a master at reading people.

Her voice goes impossibly quieter, and I know we've made a wrong turn in forcing her to tell us so much. Every fifth word, her voice loses all volume. "Mama and I were taking the bus home from my college graduation a couple years ago. I guess the semitruck didn't see us. He rammed into the bus from the side and tipped it over. Fourteen people died, including Mama." She comes to the end of her napkin, and her words stop when she runs out of pieces to tear and line up.

I hand her mine, and she finds her voice again.

I helped her find the freedom to speak, and I love it.

Her eyes flick up to me. "That's when I saw your twin. Santiago. He pulled only me from the wreck. He knew about the strength stuff. So, the three of you, Santiago and my mom."

She looks at me and my heart stutters. Though I know my signs don't mean anything to her, it's the only language I have, so I go with it, mouthing as clearly as I can, *"I was in captivity up until two-and-a-half years ago. We weren't allowed out of the cave. Santiago never set foot on concrete without an order from Father. I would have known about you, about the mission of them sending Santiago to you. I don't understand."*

She shakes her head. "Okay, I caught, like, half of that. I didn't know Santiago at the time, and I haven't seen him since. He lowered himself into the tipped-over bus, walking over bodies like he was looking just for me."

Then she goes silent. I know there's more, and I can see she wants to tell us. She's just working up the nerve.

The waitress brings us our food but none of us acknowledges her, not even Rafi, who usually has a wink and a quip for anything in a skirt.

Santiago. My brother was sent on a secret mission from

the Kalku? Since when would that have happened? Why didn't he tell me? We were never allowed out of the cave.

Sweat beads on the nape of my neck. I don't understand.

Adelita motions to my clothes. "I didn't recognize the similarities at first."

Rafi fills in the gaps. "Santiago has been dead for a while now. The Kalku killed him."

Adelita pauses her own pain and reaches over to place her hand atop mine. For all the confusion I feel, that small weight settles my storm of questions. "He had golden eyes, like yours. Kindness in them that can't be faked, just like you." Her mouth pulls to the side, and I can tell she's trying to remember Santiago exactly.

I take a bite of my dry toast, which breaks up the seriousness for a beat.

Rafael's mouth pulls to the side as he scolds me. "At least put something on that, Santos. There's no joy in that mouthful. Everything should have a little joy." He nudges the caddy with packets of jam stacked high, silently pushing me to break a rule that doesn't have good reason to shatter.

I frown at him, knowing exactly what he's doing. *"Sugar is weakness. Father said so."*

Cruz meets my eyes with a seriousness that tells me he's going to deliver the same speech he does whenever I mention life in the cave. "You aren't with the Kalku anymore. You're a free man, Santos. The Cave Master is not your father anymore. My dad is yours because you're my brother now."

Adelita's eyes bounce back and forth between us, cataloging things in ways I wish she wouldn't. Maybe she thinks I'm naïve or stupid. Maybe she thinks I'm a rabid, wild man.

I decide she should know who she's traveling with. We've expected her to divulge too many things. I need her to know why I am the way I am, in case I do something wrong that scares her. *"I'm not like them,"* I admit to her.

She's still got her hand atop mine. On top of the table. Where anyone can see her fraternizing with the likes of me.

"I'm not translating that," Rafael rules. "You're just like Cruz and me. We have the same address, carry the same workload. Same last name, even. We're the same."

It's defiance, plain and simple. It's sweet, but untrue.

I turn in the booth to face Adelita so she can read my lips. *"Santiago and I were stolen by the Kalku when we were babies, raised to be protectors of their cave. Over and over, Santiago and I were trained to be the best weapons possible to defend the cave. No sugar, no alcohol, no smoking, no women. Exercise regimen for the first hour of the day, language studies for the second hour, practice magic until Father was satisfied, and then tend to the needs of the elders. Laundry, cleaning, cooking, securing the cave as best we could."*

When I stop, Rafael has his eyes on his food but he's not eating. He doesn't like talk about my life in the cave. My parents never stepped forward to claim me when I was liberated, and neither did his. Either my parents are dead or they don't want to be associated with someone who lived as long as I did with the enemy.

Rafi's parents didn't want him back when he was liberated at five years old. They said he'd been polluted and ruined by the Kalku, I believe he told me.

"When Santiago made a mistake in his lessons, they punished me instead." I tap the side of my face, showing her the scars without embarrassment.

In truth, I'm not embarrassed by them. They're signs that I love my brother, that I would do anything for my family. They're not my shame; they're my honor.

Then I tell her, *"I wish I knew why he came to you, or*

anything about it, but I don't. Santiago pulled you out of that bus for a reason, and I trust him."

Her brows crease with concern. "He picked me up and carried me out of the bus. When he set me down on the pavement, he…" she squirms and rubs the nape of her neck. "That was all. I never saw him again." She tears the rest of her napkin and goes silent until I hand her Rafael's to maim.

The toast in my mouth tastes like sand, my world going still as I contemplate all the ramifications of what it could mean that my brother knew about Adelita, that the Kalku knew and they must've sent him to save her.

And I knew none of it.

12

DIFFERENT NOW

CRUZ

I don't think Santos realizes his fork is bent in half until Rafael pries it from his grip.

"Santiago saved you from the bus crash," Rafi says. "He must've told you his name. What else did he say?"

Her cheeks get this brush of pink. She rips at her stinking napkin like she's trying to figure out the meaning of life via the napkin's destruction. "He explained that I'm different now. But it came with a caveat."

"Which is?" Honestly, it's like pulling teeth to get this woman to talk. She's infuriating.

Her chin dips and her voice drops. For a second, I visualize reaching across the table to shake her shoulders.

I can only just make out her confession when it finally comes. "I'm the strongest person in the world, but Santiago told me he was making it so that I'll only be as strong as I am gentle." Then she drops the napkin on the table and cradles her face in her hand. "That sounds so arrogant! I'm sorry. It's just what Santiago told me. And I'm not even sure it's true. I mean, yes, I'm strong now, but I just..." Her eyes dart guiltily around the diner before she drags her thumb across her throat. "That's not gentle, what I did to those Kalku guys. I should only be as strong as I am gentle, so I don't think the blessing Santiago gave me is holding up."

Rafi's mouth pops open, and a stream of nonsense questions spill out. "How much can you bench? How far can you throw a ball? Can you lift a car?"

I hold up two fingers to dismiss Rafi's useless interrogation to bring us back to logic. "Okay, so after Santiago came to you, blessed you and explained it, then what?"

"Can we not do this? I mean, it's my personal life and I don't know you."

Rafi holds up his hand. "I last dreamt about a three-way between me, this woman I've been with a couple times named Gloria, and Cruz. There, now you know a little about my personal life. It can't possibly be as bad as that was. Super awkward. Cruz is about as bad in bed in my dreams as you can imagine."

My head whips to Rafi, my upper lip curled in a grimace. "Gross!" It takes one shove to topple him off the bench, which he deserves for saying something so asinine.

Rafi chuckles as he rights himself and climbs back into the booth. "If it helps, you were a very tender lover. Awkward, but tender."

I honestly don't know what to do with Rafi when he goes off the rails like this. "Stop being annoying."

For some reason, Rafi's stupid jokes get her smiling, and she starts talking.

Huh.

"The next morning, I slapped my alarm clock to turn it off and it shattered. My strength went from dangerous to off the charts. So I have to be more careful now. I don't know if I can lift a car; I've never attempted it. I'm too busy trying not to accidentally hurt anyone."

That explains why she throws a punch like she's never hit

anyone in her life, yet can dent a man's skull with her limited skill.

When her cheeks go pink again, I pick up my burger and start eating. "There's more. Out with it."

She won't look at any of us. "He drew a design on my hands. Santiago. While he was talking to me."

Before I can ask what kind of design, Santos turns his hand from beneath hers atop the table and looks pointedly at his palm.

"You want me to draw on your hand?"

Rafi pulls a pen from his pocket. "Draw what Santiago doodled on your hand."

Santos nods once, his face stony. This is the most conversation we've had about his deceased brother since Santiago died. He doesn't like to discuss his twin's death. Can't blame him for that.

"I mean, I don't know. I was too rattled to pay much attention to the design. I'd just been in a bus crash, and I was in shock."

She places her hand atop Santos' again and his whole body melts for her. He was rigid with tension a breath ago, but the second she touches him, his shoulders go concave and he slides closer. His chest seems to draw itself to her, and she leans in without that annoying debate she always does over every little allowance. She doesn't hesitate so much with Santos.

I make a note to have *him* extract information from her next time.

Judging by the way he looks at her as if she's the prettiest thing on two legs, I'm guessing he'll be opposed to using force.

Still, I can't have someone in our group that I can't trust.

I hope we don't have to do everything the hard way when it comes to her.

13

CORRUPTING SANTOS

SANTOS

"The ride to the curse tree in Buckley takes two days," Cruz informs Adelita. She sighs at the long car ride but doesn't otherwise complain. She's used to a five-minute trip to work and back, not days across the country all to see a tree with a bunch of axes stuck in it.

I hope it takes a week. When she's sure Cruz is hypnotized by the road and Rafi's asleep, she rests her hand in the seat between us. It's an invitation for me to link my littlest finger around hers.

Whenever I do it, she smiles and refuses to look at me. I've never made a woman bashful before, and I love it. I feel so powerful and strong.

And confused. Why doesn't she look at me like I'm a savage? Maybe she still doesn't understand my upbringing.

She is so sweet, holding on to my finger like it's some scandal she doesn't want Cruz or Rafael to see. Not that I blame her. She doesn't know them.

Plus, it's anybody's guess what will provoke Cruz's temper on any given day.

Traffic gets more condensed as evening nears, so Cruz pulls off to refuel.

"Do you want me to take a turn driving?" Adelita offers.

"Why? Do you think you'll be able to get us all the way back to your precious home without me realizing where you're taking us?"

My internal groan matches Rafael's loud noise of exasperation as he stretches. "She's offering because she's nice, dummy. She doesn't know you're a control freak." Then Rafi explains to Adelita, "Cruz won't let anyone else drive. He's got issues."

"I need to stretch my legs." It's her way of letting us know she's had it with Cruz, but is too polite to go head-to-head with him.

She grabs her purse and steps out of the car. Before Cruz can tell me to watch her, I'm hot on her heels. Though she can clearly take care of herself in a fight, she's still to be protected.

It's an oddly pleasant experience, walking into the convenience store with her. The clerk looks up, and I'm guessing he surmises we're a couple. The thought makes me smile as she picks an aisle and browses through the selection of nuts and snacks.

"What are you grinning about?" she asks curiously.

I shove my hands in my pockets and shrug, unable to help myself. We even match, thanks to Cruz picking out the same black t-shirt and jeans uniform we all wear. "Everything is to be studied," Father used to say. I take it to heart with Adelita, and catalog what items she frowns at and which she selects. A packet of chili candies that the package guarantees are "screaming hot," a sleeve of caramels, trail mix and a bottle of water. A smile builds with each item she chooses.

Then her pleasant expression falls with a sudden crash. "Oh, you don't eat sugar. I forgot."

Though she looks only mildly put out about it, something in me shifts. I want to give her whatever it is that'll make her smile again, even if it's as monumental as me going against Father's edicts.

I sign and mouth "I'll try it," and just like that, she lights up like a Christmas tree. She's got one of those smiles that makes the whole room fade away, and leaves you with the impression that the world might not be such a grim place after all. I don't know how she does it.

Heart-shaped. That's what her mouth is like. Not like the real hearts Father used to carve out of people's chests and boil in our stew to give us extra endurance. The kind of hearts that the children in Cruz's village draw on paper and giggle about. It's a pretty shape, and I find I have a hard time focusing when her lips move.

"Really? I mean you don't have to, but I think you'll like this. Oh! This gets to be your very first sugar? You'll be spoiled for life."

Then she does something so endearing, I'm not sure I'll be of any use if she actually does need protecting.

Adelita squeezes my hand.

Anyone can see. Like I'm a normal man and she's happy to be near me. I'm a ball of nerves and joy when she pulls me over to the machine Cruz sometimes uses when he's been driving too long. Only she doesn't go for the coffee. She deposits her treasures in my hands and grins up at me before she turns and fixes four hot chocolates with varying flavors mixed together.

She secures them in a cardboard carrier but before she can lift them, my body moves to pick them up for her.

"You don't have to do that. Thank you. But now you're carrying everything. That's hardly fair."

I shrug, letting her know this is how it's going to be. I'm not sure I'm capable of holding myself back if she needs something, even a thing as small as carrying her trinkets. She lets me come near her, which is no small blessing.

If she keeps looking at me like that, she can have whatever she likes, as far as I'm concerned.

I scare the women in the village. They know too much of Kalku culture and still too little to trust me. They don't like to look me in the eye, and whenever I enter a room, they stop talking and usually find a polite way to leave.

It's better than the shrieking they used to do when I was first brought to the village.

But Adelita makes eye contact. She beams at me with this light that knocks the air from my chest. She doesn't assume I'm savage or too dangerous to come near. In fact, she opted to stay in the same room as me last night—actually chose me.

No one chooses me.

Even in the Kalku, Santiago was selected for the more prestigious displays of magic. I was reserved for torture and grunt work.

No wonder they didn't tell me there was a woman who needed tracking, and gave Santiago that task instead.

I'm so lost in my thoughts that I don't see her card until it's nearly in the machine. I shake my head and set down the items, holding my hand up to her to stop her from doing something detrimental to our mission. We need to get to the curse tree in Buckley undetected. That means no cards. Nothing that can be tracked.

I try to sign as much to her, but she doesn't understand my urgency. She thinks I'm trying to be chivalrous and not let her pay, which is something I kick myself for not doing.

I know she'll be miffed, but I take her card from her hand and put it back in her purse. I pay for the food with cash, then grab it all before she can get too frustrated in front of the cashier.

When we get to the car, Rafael explains it all for me, which lessens my angst a bit at going over her head.

Her shoulders slump. "Oh, I didn't realize. I don't have cash on me. I can't stop at an ATM and withdraw anything? At some point I need to like, eat and buy a change of clothes."

Obviously I'll buy her whatever she needs. Whatever she wants. Does she not know that?

But Cruz beats me to it. "We travel with more cash than anyone could ever need, so if you want something, say so." He meets her eyes in the rearview mirror. "I know you don't want to hear that, but whenever we pull someone from a bad situation, this is standard. No one expects you to have a ton of cash on you, so don't let your pride get all wounded over it."

Oddly, it's the nicest thing he's said in a while. Odder still is that she seems to hear it, nodding once to let us know she won't fight us on this. "Thank you. Can we at least keep a tally of my expenses, so that when all this blows over, I can pay you back?"

"No," Cruz rules unapologetically and without equivocation.

"What'd you get us, *linda*?" Rafael turns in his seat as Cruz starts driving.

Her sweet smile brightens the entire interior of the car even as the sun sets outside. "Only the best hot chocolate you'll ever have in your life."

"Hot chocolate?" Rafi smirks at her cuteness. "You must think I'm a little boy still. We usually just get coffee."

"At night?" She shakes her head as she carefully pops open the lids. "It makes me sad that you don't think like a little boy anymore. You've been on the job too long if that's true."

Rafi lets out an airy laugh through his nose. Of all of us, he's the least adult.

A beautiful woman is making me a drink. That's not something that happens to me every day. Eva, Cruz's sister, brought me water once when she was bringing Rafael some wine.

When I was first rescued and brought into the village, Eva was nice to me because her brother was firm that I would be a permanent fixture in the Cáceres tribe. Going against Cruz just isn't something people are willing to do outright. I remember Eva's hand shaking when she handed me the water. The daughter of the chief, terrified of me.

Santos the Savage.

Eva hugs me now, but it took a long time for her to get used to me. Even though she tells people I'm her brother, I know I'll always be the outsider—the prop that proves rehabilitation is possible for those they rescue. Most other refugees aren't allowed to stay, but are shipped back to their old lives.

Except I had nothing to return to.

Cruz made an impassioned case for my citizenship, but in the end, it took the chief adopting me for the tribe to allow me to stay.

They don't exactly warm to outsiders. Much less if the person in question is liberated from an enemy's clutches. The enormous wall around their village is supposed to keep people like me out. It's their point of pride, some of them, a thing that can look to and draw comfort, certain that no one is polluting their way of life.

Except for me.

Adelita doesn't hesitate when she hands me the lids to hold. In fact, she smiles a little when her finger brushes my palm.

Rafi squints in her direction. "What are you doing to those? Cruz has a thing about being poisoned."

"Seriously? You're worried about me poisoning you?"

She's not as afraid of us, now that her secret is out. "If I wanted to kill you, I could just crush your throat." When this doesn't alleviate anyone's concerns, she sighs. "Santos is watching me. You're safe from the big, scary therapist."

Rafael chuckles. "Good to know." He claps Cruz on the shoulder. "How much longer till we're safe enough to stop for the night, oh fearless leader?"

Cruz isn't choking the steering wheel, so I know he's not stressed about a tail. The traffic is thicker than he'd like for this time of the evening, but he's not overly aggressive about it. "Honestly, we should probably break for the night soon. We're not getting anywhere in this mess." His eyes flick to a lit-up sign near the freeway's entrance. "There's some big concert in town. That's what's slowing everything down."

Adelita opens the hot chili candies and drops six in each cup, and then two caramels before refastening the lids. I quirk my eyebrow at her mischievous grin. "You won't regret it. Not to brag, but I make the best gas station hot chocolate, like, in the universe."

When I reach for one, she inches them away with that same grin that makes me feel like I'm a teenager with possibilities, instead of an adult with inevitabilities.

"Not yet," she scolds me. "You'll burn your tongue. You have to wait twenty minutes. Gotta let the candies melt. It's worth the wait, though."

Cruz tosses over his shoulder to her as he merges toward the offramp, "Santos doesn't do sugar."

Her jaw tightens, but beyond a slight clip in her voice, she doesn't offer up willingly that Cruz is getting on her nerves. She's so very controlled. "He said he'd give it a try. He trusts me not to poison him with sweetness."

Cruz's eyes widen as they flick to me in the mirror. "So you eat sugar now, do you?"

I shrug and turn my chin toward the window to avoid his question.

Rafi answers for me. "So what if he does? Good for you, Santos. Live a little." He turns in his seat to look at Adelita. "Are you sure you were only gifted strength and not persuasion, too? Never thought I'd see the day he'd budge on that. Here's to corrupting Santos."

He chuckles but she glances up at me with a worried expression. "Am I hurting you? Am I making you do something bad? I don't want to corrupt something good."

Her words stun me so much that I gape at her innocence. Even Rafael goes silent.

My hands move slowly, and I hope she can understand the words on my lips. *I am not something good. I was corrupted from the time I was a baby. La Cucuy took me from my mother's arms, and I never saw her again.*

It's the wrong thing to say, apparently, even though it's true.

Genuine pain slashes her features, tenting her eyebrows and twisting that heart of a mouth into a grimace. "Why would you say that? It's not true, Santos. Bad people don't stitch up strangers. Bad people don't help me change my clothes in such a respectful way. Bad people don't buy me candy and hot chocolate." She shakes her head as Cruz exits the freeway and searches silently for a motel for the night. "Some people have to work harder to overcome their upbringing, is all. But you don't strike me as a man who's afraid of hard work."

Rafi's voice is rough with held back emotion when he speaks. "I hope you're listening to her, Santos."

Then she places her hand atop mine while balancing the drink carrier on her lap. I freeze because I'm afraid if I breathe, even something that small might shatter the sweetness of the moment. Real warmth flows through her and sinks into me. It's a soothing balm for the cold and cracked parts I've grown accustomed to.

For the first time in my life, I feel like being me might not always be such a terrible thing.

14

CLEANING LADY AND CRUSH
ADELITA

Cruz runs his hand over his face. "Never mind. We'll go to a different motel if you've only got one room."

The pimply twenty-something behind the counter struggles to find his voice to correct Cruz, intimidating as he always is. "I know for a fact that everything in town is booked, and the next town over. It's the big concert up at the stadium. I only have this room free because the people with the reservations just called a few hours ago. They got a flat tire and couldn't make it to the show. Shame. It's gonna be a killer performance."

Cruz's jaw tightens. "Fine. We'll take the one room, then. Got any cots?"

The younger man shakes his head. "We've got extra towels, but even those will be snatched up in a couple hours. Here. Take a few now." He goes into the backroom and returns with a stack for us, like he's cutting us some secret deal. He wants Cruz to like him, that much is certain.

Poor kid doesn't realize that Cruz's face only comes with one expression—surly control.

Santos and Rafael shoulder the bags and my purse while I

carry the hot chocolates, which are finally at the perfect drinking temperature. The room is small, barely squeezing in the advertised two queen beds. The carpet smells like the thousands of feet that have walked across this dreary maroon color.

There are fingerprints on the windows, which my mama would never have tolerated. She was the best cleaning woman in the world, and took pride in leaving each room sparklingly immaculate.

Of all the things I've been and will become, I am first and foremost my mother's daughter.

The itch to clean is strong, and combines with my fidgety energy from being cooped up in the car all day. I set the beverage caddy down and meander into the hallway, looking left and right until my eyes land on a housekeeping cart that's been left unattended.

Even the twenty feet of space is too much for the guys, so Rafael follows me out into the hallway as I lift the disinfectant and a few unused rags.

"You don't have to clean a motel before you use it, *linda*."

I keep my eyes on the supplies when the door shuts behind us, closing out the rest of the world from our quaint motel room. "I used to clean hotels with Mama. Now that I'm not bleeding all over the place, I have the brain space to worry about things like germs and unsanitary living conditions." I ignore his protest and meander into the bathroom, which is just as unkempt as I worried it might be.

Santos doesn't deserve to stay in a dirty room. He stitched me up and prepared to use his body as a human shield when we were being chased on the road. He's a good man.

It takes no time at all to spray down the sink and toilet, but when I get down on my knees to scrub the bowl, Santos nearly has a heart attack. He barrels into the tight space, shaking his head as he lifts me up. Then he disappears with the rag and the bottle to toss them into the maid's cart before he stomps back inside, visibly upset.

His hands are flicking a mile a minute, but I'm not getting a word of it as I wash my hands and arms. It's hard to do things like that one-handed, so I manage to make a bigger mess than I was hoping, splashing water on the sink and getting a little on my sleeve.

Santos snaps out of his frustration when he sees me angling my body so I can get my slinged arm under the flow. Then he harrumphs and clears the gap between us, lathering up his hands so he can wash my filthy parts.

He won't look at me, but I can tell I've done something to upset him. How maddening it must be to have too many things to say and not be able to communicate any of them. He slaps his hands twice, and Rafael comes to stand in the doorway.

He signs to Rafael, who frowns. "Santos, it's okay that she's cleaning. It doesn't mean she's a slave. It means she's thoughtful."

This is apparently not what Santos wants to hear. His hands are getting more emphatic, his pretty mouth drawn in a tight line.

Gosh, he's handsome.

Rafael sighs. "Well, I don't know what to tell you, man. She's not going to go for it." When Santos jabs his finger in my direction, Rafael shoots me an apologetic look. "Santos doesn't want you cleaning toilets. If you want something scrubbed, you're to tell him, and he'll do it."

Santos smacks the flat of his palm to his chest to punctuate Rafael's words.

My mouth draws to the side. "I didn't pull my stitches, if that's what he's worried about. I was careful."

"It's not that. Well, it's not *just* that. It's his culture. Santos was raised to understand that cleaning is done by slaves, not proper members of society. It's a whole big thing. If I were you, I'd take it as a compliment and chalk it up to one of the many differences you'll have to adjust to while you're traveling with Santos. Some things can't be easily deprogrammed."

I'm not sure how to take any of it, but when I see Santos is visibly upset, I decide making him understand my logic isn't as important as his insistence that this is the way the world works. "I'm sorry, Santos. I didn't mean to upset you."

He meets my gaze for a few beats. The gold of his eyes reflects the light as if he travels with pure sunshine that comes from inside of his body. The gold beams out at me whenever I have need for something beautiful. I can tell by his tensed throat and the dare in his set jaw that he's amping up to fend off my forthcoming arguments.

When I don't present him with one, his shoulders deflate and he signs to Rafael while mouthing, *I'm going for a walk.* Then he moves toward the door.

I expect him to leave but it's like he can't. He stops, turning a few times in my direction, then away, then back again until he signs to Cruz something about me. I've learned that his sign for me is a sort of fist that circles around his face.

Cruz's eyes flick in my direction before he nods and signs back something also about me.

"Hey!" I don't realize I'm irritated until my volume raises higher than normal. "None of this secret language stuff right in front of me. I know you're talking about me, so either someone needs to translate or else start teaching me sign language."

Rafael sniggers while Santos' neck shrinks at my scolding. "I'll teach you a few words, *viento*. And while you're learning,

I'll translate." Santos takes this as his cue to exit, leaving Rafael, Cruz and I staring at each other.

Rafael kicks off his boots. He speaks slower now, so I can tell he's tired. "Santos was saying that he's going on a walk, but he doesn't want you out of our sight. Then he changed his mind and said he didn't want to leave. Cruz told him to chill out and go, so he went." Rafael grins at me as he scratches his five o'clock shadow. "If you didn't catch the subtext of that, you're in luck, because I also happen to be an excellent interpreter for subtext. Santos has it bad for you. He's never looked twice at a woman before, so tread lightly."

My fingers find each other so my thumb can rub over my fingernails to soothe my nerves. "Meaning?"

Cruz stands and fishes out a set of clean clothes from his backpack. "Meaning you don't know how bad off Santos was when we found him, and how little he knows about the world still. My uncle told me to get rid of him, that people like Santos can't be rehabilitated."

Immediately, a sense of disdain for his uncle cements in my psyche. "'People like Santos'? What's that supposed to mean?"

Cruz's eyes darken as memories of long past glint with unmistakable pain. "Santos is a Cadejo. Did you notice his yellow eyes?"

I bristle, and though I don't want to get caught up in an argument with Cruz, for some reason I can't be silent. "Not yellow. His eyes are golden. Yellow makes it sound like he's evil or something. Gold is hopeful. Gold is beautiful."

Heat creeps into my cheeks when Rafi sniggers. He covers his mouth to keep his comments about my blatant crush to himself, thank goodness.

Cruz doesn't do emotion, so he skips over my awkward comment altogether. "Golden eyes are the sign of a Cadejo. A shapeshifter. Those are made, not born, and only the Kalku know how to do that sort of thing. It's barbaric, what they put the shifters through. The Kalku had him and his brother since he was a baby, training Santos to be their slave and also their greatest weapon. He cleaned, cooked and did everything the Kalku demanded. He was their tool, Adelita. His brother Santiago had the gift of cursing, so he was more useful to them. They treated Santiago better. Occasionally let him eat at the table. Santos still won't eat at our family's table, even though we've had him a couple years now. Santos has the gift of healing, which isn't as useful to them. He had to heal his abusers, Adelita. Wrap your mind around that." Cruz pinches the bridge of his nose, drawing attention to the purple shadows under his eyes. "I was raised as a soldier, but the twins were raised as weapons. Neglected, abused, and with a narrow understanding of the world."

Cruz rubs the nape of his neck. I'm shocked he hasn't clammed up yet. I'm still as a statue so I don't disturb whatever clarity Cruz has reached to be able to speak this much without saying anything overtly nasty.

Cruz massages his forearm with clumsy fingers. I can tell he's overly tired. "When we freed him, Santos attached pretty hard to Rafi and me. He didn't have anyone else."

When Cruz goes silent, Rafael picks up the thread. "A member of our tribe—the Cáceres tribe—was causing problems in the village, stirring up talk that Cruz is gone too much to be useful to the tribe and should be replaced. He did one of those hyper-macho bumps to Cruz's shoulder when he walked by, and Santos snapped." Rafael raises his arm. "Stabbed the poor idiot through the arm he knocked Cruz with to teach him a lesson."

When Cruz interjects, it's as if he assumes I'm judging Santos and he needs to defend his friend. It's sweet, the way the three of them stand up for each other. "Santos means well but he doesn't understand everything yet. So be careful.

He's getting attached to you, which means he might stab anyone who frowns in your direction. He's not exactly popular back in the village. They think he's a savage."

I take his warning with gratitude, factoring this new information into my view of the man who rescued and healed me. If they're worried about Santos being protective of me, then they clearly don't see how strong my attachment to him is becoming. I don't like to think of people viewing him as a savage. He's clearly not.

I should keep my mouth shut about my opinions, but the second my lips part, my education spills out. "That's ridiculous—people calling Santos a savage. Savages care nothing about the whole, only their immediate id." When my explanation goes over their heads, I choose better words. "They're all impulse and no control, but Santos is nothing like that."

He's kind to me, caring about the smallest ache and pain.

I straighten as much as I'm able. "I don't think I'll get on well in your village, if Santos is ostracized. He's clearly a good person."

Rafael's eyebrows lift in amusement. "Well, well. It looks like we don't have to worry about Santos' crush being one-sided."

My cheeks flush afresh. "I don't know what you're talking about. I'm just saying he's obviously not... He's..." I tug on my fingers over and over. "We can be done talking about this now."

Cruz is equally as shocked as Rafael at my assessment of Santos. "That's a lot better of a response than I was expecting. If I can give you one piece of advice, it would be to tread lightly and be patient. Santos has no idea what he's doing. The Kalku don't allow women in their tribe, so he's a bit of a newbie to the whole thing."

I bite down on my lower lip, wishing I wasn't getting relationship advice from Cruz, of all people. "Thanks. Now can we be done talking about this? I think we've got bigger things to discuss than whether or not Santos likes me."

The two men respond as one voice. "He does."

I rub my temple, ready to be done with this whole conversation. "Moving on. How long is this whole getting-the-bad-guys-to-leave-me-alone thing going to take? I don't want to lose my job. My patients depend on me." I shudder to think what my Friday morning regular with abandonment issues will do if I'm not there, come her next appointment.

Cruz's face goes stony as he stretches his legs. "Maybe you didn't understand how bad things are when I told you the Kalku are after you. They're not just a few idiots we can stamp out when they get annoying. It's a huge tribe, and they're loyal to a man that's more powerful and farther-reaching than anything we can contain. They won't stop until they've got ahold of everything they want. And once they do, they'll want more assets, and still more. This doesn't end."

Cruz rolls his shoulders back, and suddenly he looks enormous, towering over me like some giant authoritarian figure I'm supposed to cower to.

My heart picks up its pace, unused to men laying down any sort of law with me. I never met my father, and spent most of my free time with the genteel Tomás, so I don't know what to do in a situation like this.

Cruz takes in my discomfort and steps back so as not to purposefully intimidate me with his overwhelming stature.

His voice is quiet but delivers a firm command that doesn't invite my input. "You cannot go back to your life. Probably not ever."

15

ERASED WITH EASE
ADELITA

Santos returns before we can get into a big argument about it all. He's got takeout and a bag from a store I noticed on the strip behind the motel. There's a terse edge to his jaw but his shoulders are relaxed and he doesn't look palpably upset anymore.

"Did you get me something pretty?" Rafael teases, poking inside the bag curiously.

Santos shoves him away and sets the bag on the bed that's not occupied by Cruz's things. He points to me. He signs while Rafael translates, "Clean clothes for you. If I got the sizes wrong, I'll get you something else."

When you live alone and you have no family, it's the little things that stick to your skin like loneliness. Aside from the clothes I'm currently wearing, no one's bought me clothes in a couple years. Not new socks. Not a corny t-shirt from a vacation. Nothing. If I need something, I go buy it myself, or I make it, like I did my cardigan (which is now who knows where, bloodied and torn).

I know it's not a gift. This is necessity, this bag of clothes, but I let myself believe it's a present just for me for no reason other than to make my life a little bit brighter. "Thank you. I'm sure they'll fit great."

"You look like a therapist when you do that," Rafael comments.

My nose crinkles at his assessment. "And what does a therapist look like?"

Rafi motions to my face. "Like you're taking the clothes and parsing them for subtext."

I frown at him. "Well, subtext is like, half my job."

Rafael moves to stand in front of me, bobbing on the balls of his feet like a little boy in line for ice cream. "Do me!"

"Pardon me?"

"Shrink my head. Size me up. Give me your professional evaluation, Doc."

I chuckle at his enthusiasm. "First off, I have my master's, not my doctorate. Second, I'm sure you don't want that. I'm not in the habit of giving evaluations in front of other people, and certainly not outside the office."

Well, I try not to do that aloud, at least.

Rafael shields me from the bag of takeout. "Please? I've never been to therapy before."

I snort. "I'm utterly shocked to hear that." When it's clear Rafael won't relent, I sigh. "Alright, but I could be wrong. Understand that, alright? It's just my at-a-glance opinion. And a flash diagnosis is nothing like treatment, so this does nothing, except perhaps add some self-awareness into the mix. What you do with it is on you."

If Rafael were a dog, his tail would be wagging. "Lay it on me."

I can't help my grin. I miss working. "I rely on a very old and trusted system called the Enneagram. It uses numbers to sum up a person's motivations. Rafael, you are a seven on the Enneagram."

"That's good, right? It sounds like it's the best one." He grins at his brothers. "See? I'm already winning."

"You can't win the Enneagram. One number isn't better than another."

"Tell that to non-sevens."

"You are ridiculous."

"Ridiculous times seven?" His eyebrows dance.

I motion to his form. "Sevens are called Enthusiasts. They're fun-loving, are often scattered and lack lasting focus. They're spontaneous and are willing to try anything once, so they end up being quite versatile."

Rafael balks at me. "Well, that's spot on." He covers his chest as if he's shielding his breasts from view. "I'm scandalized that you've summed me up so shamelessly. I feel naked now."

"Which is why I only do private therapy sessions."

Just like that, Rafael's pointing to Cruz. "Do Cruz! Do Cruz!"

"Eight," I say without flare or the ability to hold back. There is no question about that. Within the first five minutes, his eight-ness made itself known.

"Ha!" Cruz says, jutting out his chin in Rafi's direction. "Eight is better than seven. I'm winning."

"It's not... There's no winning in the Enneagram," I repeat, but it falls on deaf ears. "Cruz, you're what's called the Challenger. You're powerful, dominating and confrontational. You're willful to a fault. When you're healthy, you can be all those things as well as considerate of other people. When you're not healthy, you're..." I motion to his form.

Rafael finishes my thought. "...an ass?" When I don't respond, Rafi waves his hand in the air dismissively. "You don't have to agree aloud. Keep your heart beating if I'm right."

I tilt my head at his antics.

Santos shirks back when Rafael's attention falls on him. Of course he does.

I lower my voice. "Santos, you're a five on the Enneagram. You're what's referred to as the investigator. You're intense, cerebral and perceptive. You're also secretive and you seek isolation rather than belonging."

The room falls silent. I've done it again. Miss Life of the Party brings the levity to a crashing halt with her work talk.

Santos finally signs and mouths, *What are you?*

I'm a six, but they don't need that information. "I'm a therapist. It doesn't matter what I am. My patients matter."

Rafael casts me a skeptical "hmm," while Santos stares at me as if he's trying to see right through to my very soul.

Santos sets the takeout bag on the uneven table and motions for me to grab some food. When Rafael reaches inside, he smacks Rafi's hand away and indicates I should choose something first.

My eyes dart to Cruz, who raises his hands to indicate this is what he was talking about.

"Thanks, Santos. Did you already eat?" I fish out two tacos from the stack of probably thirty.

Santos shakes his head and offers the bag to Cruz next. It's deliberate, this shift in hierarchy.

After Rafael's taken what he wants, finally Santos grabs a few for himself. It's the same in the way the seating arrangement works. There are two chairs at the rickety table, and Santos doesn't even consider taking one. He kicks off his boots and sits sideways on the bed, leaning his back on the wall that the queen frame has been pushed up against.

I hand out the gas station hot chocolates, which are at the perfect drinking temperature now. I munch on my taco while I wait for the obligatory moans of satisfaction I know are coming.

Rafael does not disappoint. "Woah! That's the best drink I've had in a long time. What did you do to this?"

I shrug, smirking at my prowess. "Nothing too crazy. I'm glad you like it."

Cruz sips his, and then takes a long drink, which I think is a compliment.

I hold mine, waiting for Santos' reaction. He eyes the tall paper cup warily, and I can see the debate plain on his face. It's a big leap, this drink. The fact that he's never had sugar before is something I love that I can be part of. I get to be a mile-marker in his journey.

"Santos, are you alright?" I ask quietly as I sit on the bed across from his. "I shouldn't have said your Enneagram number in front of the guys."

But he waves off my concern and mouths, *I don't care about that.* It's the cup his eyes are focused on. He casts me a worried look before sniffing the cup. He studies Cruz and Rafael for signs of… I'm not sure exactly. He's very worried about the whole thing, and I realize maybe I've pushed him a little too far.

I stand, putting my food on the nightstand so I can lean towards him. "Never mind. You don't have to drink it. I can tell it's upsetting you. I shouldn't have asked you to do something you clearly don't want to do. I'm sorry."

But before I can arrest the cup from his hand, he tips it to his lips, obstinate that I not take it away.

Rafael cusses in astonishment while Cruz pauses with his taco halfway to his mouth. Both men gawk at the strange sight as Santos imbibes his very first mouthful of sugar.

"Did you really just do that?" Rafael spouts with wide eyes.

"What do you think?" I ask, still standing in the space between the two beds. "Did you like it?"

Santos takes another drink before he smiles up at me.

Then, as if there's liquid courage in the cup, he jerks his chin to the space on the bed next to him with a confidence that didn't exist ten seconds previously.

His smile leaps onto my face. Maybe it's a small thing, to be the person who introduces Santos to sugar, but in my heart, I label it as a true moment and take him up on his offer to sit with him. In therapy, this might even be considered a breakthrough: saying farewell to tenants of your old life you thought you'd always adhere to, and trading them in for new rules that you craft yourself.

I eat semi-alone nearly every day. The three other therapists in the building take different lunch hours. Tomás took his lunch hour with me, but he was usually called away before I could polish off half my meal. Alone for breakfast, many lunches, and dinner.

I'm so happy to be invited in that I have to remind myself not to cuddle into Santos' side. He looks adorable, sipping the hot chocolate with a curious smile teasing his lips.

Cruz and Rafael talk about the Kalku's possible next move, but Rafael's eye catches on us when Santos touches the outside of his foot to mine after I climb atop the mattress. I sit sideways on the bed next to him and munch on my taco. It's so innocent, so sweet. I love the small bits of contact he offers me, and how easy it all comes. We're not doing anything risqué, but it feels intimate, his littlest toe against mine through the shield of our socks.

If this is how I finally find myself a friend to eat meals with, I'll take it.

Santos casts me furtive smiles between bites, showing off just how handsome he is. His skin is a darker brown than mine, and I love the way it plays off the curve of his pink-ish lips. His black hair swishes along his jawline, showing off his boyish waves that are just long enough to sway when he turns his head too fast, but not too long to be scraggly. He's all muscle, thick-chested with a lean waist.

I don't often get to be this near men of his hotness caliber, and it's making me a klutz with my dinner. I spill a few bits of lettuce on the comforter, but manage not to make too big a fool of myself while I finish my meal. Eating a taco one-handed is hard.

On my last bite, I escape to the shower with my clean clothes, worried I'll say something stupid to Santos. It's easier to hide out under the warm spray, so I do my best to enjoy the reprieve from his covert smiles and bashful gestures.

It's hard to dress myself after I dry off, but I don't think I can stand Santos helping me figure out my clothes again. The sizes aren't too off, and my arm is a little more flexible than it was this morning. I only wince a little when I thread my injured arm through.

The guys don't believe in pajamas, apparently, because Santos got me jeans and a new black t-shirt to wear to bed, which matches the guys.

When I trade places with Santos, he gives off this impish vibe that I'm wearing the clothes he picked out. Luckily he shuts himself in the bathroom before I say anything too stupid.

Cruz takes his phone from his pocket and hands it to me. "It's time. Call whoever might come looking for you and tell them you've moved. You can give a fake forwarding address if you need."

My mouth falls open in stunned silence before I assemble a few words. "What are you talking about? I'm only on this trip with you guys until the Kalku stop looking for me. I'm not going to erase myself from my life."

"And when do you think it might be that the Kalku accept defeat? They're not a small band of thieves, Adelita.

They're ruthless, and they won't stop until they have you. You can't go back. Not soon. Not ever. We just went over this."

My food sits like a brick in my stomach. "I'm not defense-less, you know. I can fight back if they come for me."

"I've seen that, yes. But those were a handful of soldiers. They have more, and you're untrained. If you go back to your life, everyone you love will be in danger. Is that what you want?"

It's then I realize that I don't have anyone I love in my life. Not really. My love stopped when my mama died. Though, I suppose I don't want anything bad to happen to Tomás or the rest of my colleagues and patients. I care for their wellbe-ing, but it's not the same as love.

As a six on the Enneagram, it's no wonder why I've felt adrift. I've had no one to share reliance with. No one to lean on.

It's a long bout of back-and-forth, ending with Cruz pressing his burner phone into my palm so I can make arrangements to shut my life down.

My apartment and everything in it is considered lost. My heart sinks at strangers selling off my things for pocket change. Nothing I have is all that valuable, but it's mine, and I don't want to give everything up.

When Rafael suggests hiring movers and storing my things in a storage unit, that soothes my aching heart a little. There are pictures of my mama that I don't want thrown away. Maybe I won't be able to see them for a while, but knowing they're still there helps me breathe through the process of shutting my entire life down.

My car, my apartment and my job are all lifted from my hands in the span of five minutes.

The guys have done this before—utterly deleted someone. It's all done effortlessly, taking me through the steps of closing out accounts, bowing out of my lease, and sending out movers to deal with the rest.

I'm erased with embarrassing ease.

Rafael's at least considerate of the fact that this is hard and awful, but Cruz is emotionless, pushing me to the next task and the next until no one will care that I've utterly vanished, because it's all done so seamlessly.

But *I* care.

My whole being feels weighted with despair while Cruz calls his uncle with updates.

I take the unoccupied bed and tuck myself under the covers so I can pretend I'm asleep. The guys give me my ruse, moving about the room quietly as they close out their night.

Santos emerges from the bathroom in a cloud of steam, his face falling when he sees that the sugar-laced mood has died in his absence.

"Erased her," Cruz explains, punching a hole in my chest with his callous words. "Barely took any time at all."

Maybe that was supposed to be a good thing, but it sizzles on my skin like a burn that eats away at my optimism.

Rafael's voice is quieter. "Yeah, it only took like, five minutes this time. She's a loner. No one will come looking for her, so we're in the clear to keep going."

Cruz makes a few grunting noises while he stretches. "Keep an eye on her tonight, will you? I'm turning in."

"Me too. Goodnight, *viento*."

And I realize then that Rafi's nickname for me is spot on. I do feel like the wind—cold and see-through, haphazard and directionless.

I can tell Cruz is trying to do me a solid, telling Santos to watch me, but I couldn't want anything less. I don't want Santos to know I have no deep friendships. I don't want him to see me break down in a ball of regret.

Two years slipped by without making a single lasting

connection. If I was a patient of mine, I would label myself as depressed, and on the verge of reaching an unhealthy level of antisocial tendencies.

I was supposed to get my degree, start my job and provide a better life for Mama. When she left too early, I forgot to make a new plan.

My life lived cautiously turned out to be no life at all.

16

SLEEPING WITH A WOLF
ADELITA

It's a while before Santos slips into the bed beside me, dousing me in anxiety to layer on top of my sinking depression. I wish I had it in me to be happy Cruz pushed him in my direction to sleep near me tonight, but I'm too despondent to feel like anything might be okay ever again.

I don't want Santos to know how pathetic my entire life has become. I don't know him well enough to show him my disgusting parts, which always ooze out through my tear ducts. I pray he doesn't catch sight of one large tear trailing down my face.

I roll on my side to keep my open wound from view, forgetting completely that my shoulder is still, in fact, a semi-open wound. "Ah!" I gasp, livid at my own stupidity for putting weight on such a tender area.

Santos has the lamp on in the next second. He rolls me onto my back, his face scrunched with concern. He's all business as he takes in my pain level that's clearly displayed on my face.

"I'm okay. I'm fine. I just rolled on my shoulder is all. I wasn't thinking."

Santos doesn't take my word for it, but needs to investigate for himself. The sling is removed and my elbow is straightened slowly. He sets his bag next to my head and digs through it until he pulls out a vial of something that makes me nervous.

"What is that?"

He slides it between his teeth and searches until he digs out a knife.

"Santos, I'm alright!"

He shakes his head and traces a line down his cheek while Rafael gets out of the other bed, ready to assist.

I growl in frustration, embarrassed that this is how the night is ending. "I'm not crying because I'm in pain; I'm crying because I'm sad."

Santos freezes, deflating as he tucks the medicine back in his bag. His inquiring face matches his mouthed question. *Why are you sad?*

Sad. I memorize the way his fingers flick when he makes that sign.

I shake my head and try to put on a smile. "I'm fine. Just go to sleep."

When Santos doesn't like this answer, he turns his chin to Rafael for a translation, as if I'm the mute one. I guess in this scenario, where I have answers I won't give him, I sort of am.

Rafael wastes no time ratting me out. "She's down because it took us barely any time to sever all ties. There's no one to come looking for her because she didn't have anyone in her life."

I scowl at him. "Jeez, Rafi! Thanks a lot. I don't need you to translate for me."

Rafael shrugs with a hint of apology. I see the pity in his eyes as he sits down beside where I lay. He wears a look that says he can't believe how messed up my situation is. "Put your stuff away, Santos. She doesn't need medicine. And don't worry, *linda*. You're with us now. If you were gone, we wouldn't let you fade away. We'd turn over every rock until we found you."

My breath catches in my throat. For all the asinine things Rafael says, that's actually the only one I needed to hear. "You would?"

"Of course." He slides Santos' bag to the floor and leans over his friend to resituate my pillow. "We'll take you to the Cáceres tribe and you'll have a whole village who will notice if you're gone."

I wipe away my tear and do my best to swallow any audible gulps. "Thanks."

Rafael picks up my hand, curls it into a fist and kisses my knuckles. Then he places my hand on his chest, just like I touched him when I'd been feeling his scales. He makes a contented "mm" that I think means he likes my touch. He thumbs my hip before stepping away. "Santos, tuck her in so she doesn't roll over in her sleep."

When Santos' head is turned, Rafael winks at me and returns to his bed beside Cruz.

Though Rafi was trying to throw us a bone, pushing us closer together, Santos takes the advice to heart, tucking the covers on the far side so tight that I couldn't move if I tried. Then he turns into a wolf, hops up onto the bed, turns in a circle three times and lays down next to me, cuddling up to my good arm. I'm fairly certain he takes up more space as a wolf; he's so enormous. But he's the best kind of snuggly, pressing his side to mine far easier than would happen if he was still a man.

Santos looks over to the other bed two and then three times, wary of Cruz for some reason. Just like when there was a threat on the road, Santos wraps his tail over my stomach, using his body as a shield, as if he's bracing me from a menace I don't understand. He trusts Cruz, loves him, but judging by the wary look in his eyes and the protective curve of his body as he shields me from the other bed's occupants, I wonder if I'm missing something big.

At my inquiring eyebrows, he softens. When his maw ventures out to rest against the curve of my cheekbone, a deep sigh rolls through us both.

I'm not alone tonight.

Maybe I was alone for the past two years, but in this moment, I know I don't want to keep going down that path. So many times, I let opportunity pass me by, telling myself I'd be more social when I felt better, when the pain of losing Mama was less.

I'm not sure it will ever get easier to live without her, so I hold my breath and take a chance, reaching my unharmed arm between us to brush against Santos' side under the covers.

He jerks with surprise, his eyes wide with questions. He doesn't know I need to be held, and I don't know how to ask him. So instead he snuggles closer, resting his neck over my good shoulder. His fur is warm and soft, reminding me that life won't always be harsh.

Our mirrored sighs tell me that even though it's not everything, it's every bit of something we both desperately need. His movements are slow beneath the sheets as his tail teases the few inches of skin exposed from my shirt riding up a little bit.

I love that my body trusts him.

He licks my cheek as he draws teasing lines with his tail on my forearm. The tip of his tail traces from the back of my wrist over my hand and down my pointer finger. Then all the way back up and down my middle finger. It's so soothing.

My chest finally finds a steady rhythm that lulls me to restfulness.

Santos is soundless, barely moving the mattress at all as he scoots toward me, closing the gap until there isn't an inch of space between us. I love the feel of him so near. The fact that he hasn't run away scared from my childish tears is a relief I didn't know I needed. I like Santos close, and for once, I'm going to let myself be selfish and drink in the warmth life is finally handing out to me.

My fingers thread through his fur, and my eyes drift shut. I hope that when I open my eyes again, his will be there to greet me in the morning.

17

CRUZ'S HAUNTING
ADELITA

"Stop! No!"

The sound of someone crying out in the middle of the night wakes me halfway. I can't work out how to sit up until I hear a grunt like one of the guys is being punched. Just like that, I'm sitting up, rousing Santos. "What's going on?"

Santos rolls out of bed, turns back into a man in the span of a breath, and digs in his backpack for a stick of something.

My feet are cold on the floor but they find their way to the second bed and search out the source of distress. "Cruz? Wake up, sweetheart. It's a nightmare."

I blanch at my accidental term of endearment that couldn't suit Cruz less. He is not sweet, and I am convinced he's never had a heart.

Rafi groans on the side closest to the wall, but doesn't sit up.

I touch Cruz's forehead but it doesn't calm or wake him. His chin jerks to the side while his breath syncopates. His eyes remain closed, but it's like his eyeballs are looking all around beneath his lids. I worry about what he's seeing that could amp him up like this.

Rafi finally sits up, rubbing his face in the dark of night. "You need help, Santos?"

Santos responds with a sharp shake of his head and pops a lid off the five-inch tube in his fist. On the end is a roller, which he swabs across Cruz's temples and down the sides of his neck.

The whole room suddenly smells of mint and eucalyptus, waking me more fully. I reach for Cruz's hand because even though sometimes I think he's the worst, I'm not heartless.

Rafi's sharp intake of breath gives a warning I don't heed. Yes, Cruz is a jerk, but he's suffering. Pain trumps bickering. "Adelita, let go of him! You don't understand!"

But I understand enough. I know not to end a session on time if a patient is finally opening up. I know not to leave someone to bleed out in the open, exposed to the elements of one's subconscious.

As soon as I've got a firm but soothing grip on Cruz's palm, his entire body goes limp. He falls back to a peaceful sleep, his fit leaving in a breath.

Santos is completely still, frozen in what looks like panic mingled with confusion.

Rafael's eyes are locked on the spot where my hand is joined to Cruz's. "Whoa. Did you see that? *Viento*, are you okay?"

My brows crinkle. "Of course *I'm* okay. It's Cruz who's having some sort of fit."

Then Rafi and Santos start signing to each other with tight lips and stern expressions. I know they're talking about me but I can't bring myself to voice my indignation.

Santos studies the connection with a doctor's eye as he puts the tube away.

Rafi runs his hand over his face, his eyes still wide. "That never happens."

"Cruz doesn't get nightmares usually?" I ask, rubbing my thumb over the sleeping giant's knuckles.

"No, he gets those all the time. Every night. It's just that nothing ever calms him down. Women aren't allowed near him when he's sleeping. That's why he insisted on separate rooms and was upset we couldn't get one this time. That's… wow. And they're not nightmares, really. Cruz is haunted."

I narrow my eyes at Rafi. "Haunted? That's your explanation? I'm going back to bed."

Rafael keeps his voice at a whisper. "La Sayona comes to torture Cruz in his sleep."

I look around to see if there's a bug or some other tangible pest that might explain what he's talking about, but there's nothing. "What?"

"La Sayona. I'll tell you later. Cruz doesn't like us talking about it, and he really doesn't like new people knowing he's got a problem he can't fix."

I let go of Cruz's hand and immediately he starts getting amped up again. "No. Not my fault!" His breathing turns panicked, his chest contracting violently.

I scoop his hand up, and he calms.

I test the theory, and every time I hold his hand, he goes back into a deeper sleep. When I let go, he starts murmuring and worrying without opening his eyes.

Rafi and Santos study the oddity. "What the…"

"I don't know what to do!" I whisper. "I can't stay like this all night."

Santos starts signing, motioning to his head. Rafi translates, thank goodness. "You're certain you don't feel any different in your mind? There's no foreign element that shouldn't be there?"

I can't help my grimace. "Like a voice? Like a tumor? What are we talking, here?"

"Anything at all," Rafi clarifies.

I shrug, taking care not to drop Cruz's hand. Dang, he's a heavy sleeper. "Nothing."

Rafi turns to Santos. "I don't know. I mean, if La Sayona was going to pounce, she already would have. Right?"

Santos nods once, bewildered about something I still don't understand.

Rafi's mouth tugs to the side. "So is she in the clear? Because if she is, and she can help Cruz sleep, that might be the most amazing thing in the world."

Santos signs a few more things.

Rafi scratches a spot on his shoulder and then turns his attention to me. "Switch beds with me, *viento*. When La Sayona has a hold of Cruz, no one gets any sleep. At least this way, we have a chance to salvage the night."

"Are you freaking kidding me? No way am I sleeping in a bed alone with Cruz. He's awful!"

Santos already has a plan. He shimmies past me and soundlessly moves the nightstand dividing our two beds out towards the door. Then he motions for me to sit on the bed with Cruz and Rafi while he slides our bed over, so the two Queens are bumped together.

"There's not a thing I like about this plan," I whisper with just enough punch to make it clear that this sucks.

Santos rubs his fist in a circular motion over his chest, shooting me an apologetic plea to forgive him for Cruz's unconscious neediness.

Man, he must really love Cruz to put up with this crap.

My shoulders deflate, and though I desperately want to argue for another option, this seems to be the only way to go if any of us wants to sleep tonight.

Rafi lays back down and flips the cover up over his shoulder. Santos climbs into the bed, patting the spot between him and Cruz as if this is the natural thing that should be done.

Santos looks so innocent and sympathetic to my conundrum. I don't even know how this will work, since my shoulder really can't stretch out all that far. I'm careful as I lay down, frowning at the slumbering Cruz for putting me in such an awkward position.

When the grumpy oaf rolls onto his side and rests his arm over my stomach, it's harder to stay indignant, but not impossible.

He's a little precious when his surly mouth shuts.

When my eyes flick to Santos, jerking my chin to beg him to come nearer, it's purely selfish on my part. If I'm being asked to calm Cruz down, then I don't feel too terrible when I silently ask Santos to do the same for me. He rocks closer, and the moment his fingers dance across my forearm, breathing becomes easier. Though he's not a wolf this time, I still want him near, warming my side and giving me that rare feeling of togetherness. I want Santos to chase away the loneliness that's always plagued me.

I tug Santos closer with my leg hooking over his, and he doesn't hesitate to give me what I need. If I have to be cuddled up to Cruz, at least I get to have Santos as close as I want.

I thread my fingers through his, securing him to me. His hand is pleasantly warm, just like the rest of his body. He's careful with my shoulder, making sure nothing moves too much.

Santos kisses my temple, flooding me with a fresh reminder that I'm very much attracted to this man. Santos signs something I don't understand, but I'm too tired to ask about it before I drift off to sleep.

18

ADELITA IN THE MORNING
SANTOS

I've been awake for two hours. I'm desperate to use the bathroom, but I can't bring myself to budge. Adelita's deep breaths move the comforter up and down in this calm beat that makes me feel like the world might not be such a grim place. I tried to unthread my fingers from hers, but she shifted and frowned in her sleep, as if she prefers me close.

I love that she wants me near.

And it's not just because she's unconscious and doesn't realize what she's doing. She reached for me last night. It was *my* hand she wanted to hold. She likes me pressed up against her side in my wolf form *and* my man form.

I don't even mind that Cruz needed to be near her to get a good night's sleep. I'm almost relieved Rafael and I weren't up all night listening to La Sayona torment his mind. Cruz's arm is still draped over her stomach, but it's my hand she reached for so she could sleep.

I've seen the men and women hold hands in the village. Children and parents. Little girls running through the town square while they giggle about some secret I'll never understand. No one's ever reached for my hand except my twin, and that was years ago.

I want to roll Adelita onto her side, but I know that would hurt her shoulder to move her too much. I can see it, though. I bet I could feel her heartbeat through her back, thrumming into my chest like a secret we share from the world.

I want that secret. I want to know what her heartbeat feels like.

My thumb traces up the back of her hand to rest on her wrist. It's comforting—her steady rhythm.

I think it's my contented stare that causes her lashes to flutter at the disruption. She stretches, realizing with a blush that we held hands all through the night under the covers.

Her gaze lands on mine to study my face in the morning light that's filtering through the thinned curtains. How I love the look of her all tousled and sleepy-eyed. She's too perfect to be holding my hand, yet somehow by a stroke of infinite luck, she hasn't let go. In fact, she cuddles closer, her shoulder touching mine.

"Good morning," she whispers with a small smile meant just for me.

It's too much. The whole thing is too incredible to attempt sanity. My free hand grows a mind of its own. It has to touch her. It has to know if her cheek is as soft as it was yesterday.

I move slow, giving her ample opportunity to shirk away. I'm used to women recoiling from the sight of me. Scarred face aside, I was raised by the Kalku. "Dangerous," they whisper when they skitter past me. "Savage," is usually what I hear under their breath when I walk through the village with Cruz and Rafael. Cruz always tries to convince me that my nickname is a compliment to my fighting, but "Santos the Savage" isn't easy for me to stomach.

Because it's accurate. They all know it, and so do I.

Yet Adelita seems to have no clue that she belongs with a king or someone befitting her delicate grace.

Adelita exhales contentedly when my knuckles brush her cheek. Sugar. That's what she is. She's the woman who brings hot chocolate and sweetness into my life. She feels like silk and the best kind of warmth.

Father kept sweetness away from me because he said it makes men weak.

If this is weakness, so be it.

Adelita is careful not to wake Cruz as she turns her chin more fully toward me, her nose an inch from mine.

Her breathing is steady and deep again. Parts of me I never knew what to do with awaken and lean toward her, knowing this is where I belong. Touching her soft cheek and spending my morning making sure she's relaxed and happy is the most natural thing in the world.

Just when I think I can't believe how wonderful this morning is turning out, she angles her chin up and brushes her nose across mine. It's so precious, so intimate, I can hardly believe it's meant for me.

I always assumed I was built to sleep in a cold bed by myself. But Adelita is my…

No. She is not my anything. She's too perfect to belong to me. But I belong to her, wholly and easily. I'm hers, and as long as she'll let me touch her cheek and hold her hand in bed, I'll die a happy man.

Happy. There's a word I never thought I'd put much stock in. It never mattered much before. Alive matters. Protected matters. Happy? It's always been a concept too grand to pursue. And yet, here it is, cuddled up in bed with me and nuzzling my nose as if she's convinced I'm the same brand of gentle she is.

Her torso snuggles deeper into the sheet, and the curve of her hip calls out to me. I'm pushing my luck, really pushing the edges of it to see how far it'll stretch. My hand drifts to her shoulder, trilling down her arm and hopping over Cruz's forearm to land on her ribs. And there it is, the slope of her waist that bells out at her hip. She doesn't pull away at my touch, but surprises me by lifting her knee up to hook it atop mine, drawing my thigh under hers.

My brain is firing with possibilities and impossibilities, trying to figure out which one this scenario fits into.

On the one hand, this cannot possibly be happening. She can't want to be wrapped around me so beautifully. On the other hand, here she is.

Cruz is a series of grunts and sniffs when he wakes. I don't even care that this is the background noise to our perfect morning.

It takes half a minute for his eyes to open. He stiffens once he takes in the scope of the curvy body he's been holding on to all night long. "What the... What are you doing?"

Cruz recoils from Adelita, as if she plotted and planned to get him into bed all along.

"La Sayona," Rafael mumbles, his eyes still closed. "You wouldn't calm down last night unless you were holding Adelita's hand."

Cruz goes from lidded eyes to wide awake in the span of Rafael's sentence. He shoots up out of the bed as if the mattress is on fire.

I rise slowly, holding up my hands to prove everything is fine.

Cruz isn't convinced. "Say something! Are you alright?" He tugs Adelita from my side, dragging her to the edge of the bed with such a manic look on his face that she doesn't resist. He lifts her to her knees atop the foot of the mattress, treating her body like she's a ragdoll. She lets him pry her eyes wider so he can peer inside.

"I'm alright, Cruz. My shoulder's the only problem, not my eyes."

"Your brain!" he explains without really explaining. "You… Nothing's wrong? Nothing happened?"

She gently pries herself from his grip, but she can't balance as she tries to stand from the bed, so Cruz's arms go around her waist to help her.

Her words come out before he's fully set her on her feet. "What's supposed to have happened? You're the one who had the nightmare. Is that what this is about? Are you still feeling upset about your bad dream?" She's standing in the circle of his arms as he tries to steady her. She rests her hand on his bicep, and his whole body loses all tension.

Boy do I know that feeling. There's an addiction laced in her fingertips that makes you crave more every time she touches you.

His spine relaxes and his chin droops.

Adelita's thumb massages his bicep. "It was just a dream, Cruz. It's alright."

"You're not hurt? She didn't come for you?"

Adelita's worry is nothing to Cruz's. When he glares at us for taking this chance with her life, all I feel is shame.

I should have been more careful. If La Sayona had attacked Adelita because she was near Cruz while he slept…

I do not take for granted the lucidity in her eyes, even if it's plagued with worry.

She could have died.

We could have lost her for good.

19

ADDING A FOURTH
SANTOS

*E*motion flickers in Adelita's eyes. "You dreamt I was being attacked?"

Cruz buttons his lips shut, and I can see confusion creep over his features, now that he's more fully awake. He wasn't expecting to have slept through the night, no more than he anticipated waking next to Adelita, curled up to her as if she was his shelter in his constant storm.

La Sayona left him the second Adelita touched his hand in the night. There's no mistaking the magic in that.

Still, it was a hefty chance to take. Rafi knows we screwed up by letting Adelita sleep next to Cruz, even though all signs point to her being okay. Rafi gets out of the bed and wraps his arms around Cruz, grounding him when his life veers into the deep end.

Cruz breathes deeply, allowing Rafi to calm him when he needs it. "It's alright, brother. We watched her. I wouldn't have let her sleep beside you if it wasn't clear that she would be safe." Then Rafi lays his head on Cruz's shoulder and snores loudly, letting us all know that he would rather have indulged in another hour of rest.

Cruz gives Rafi a light shove, but I can see he's still spooked by the whole thing.

I make my way to them and sign to Cruz that of course I wouldn't have allowed Adelita near him if he would put her in danger.

Rafi releases him so Cruz can hug me, gripping the back of my head as he always does when he's tightly wound. "Tell me I didn't..."

But it's clear nothing foul happened. Adelita is standing right there, looking just as lucid—albeit puzzled—as ever.

The men in the village don't hug as often as the three of us do. I don't care that our affection makes us stand out. We need it.

Cruz pulls away, his eyes climbing Adelita from toe to head. "It makes no sense. I didn't hurt you?"

A veil falls over her eyes. "You absolutely hurt me when you tore my stitches. And you hurt me every time you're mean on purpose. But last night? No, you didn't hurt me last night. You were the one in pain, not me."

"I don't understand. You didn't see... I didn't... You're not..." His jaw tightens, and I can already anticipate this taking a poor turn. "You shouldn't have touched me while I was sleeping. Is that what therapists are supposed to do? Creep up on people while they're unconscious and hold their hands without permission?"

Rafael runs a hand over his face, blinking over and over to force himself to be alert for this exchange. "None of us wants to dissect it all, so don't be a moody butthole about the whole thing. Keep your mouth shut and don't make her feel bad about it just because you're embarrassed."

"I didn't... I... Well, it's not... She shouldn't have held my hand!"

Rafi cups his hands over his mouth and releases an obnoxious "Boo!" Then he turns on his side, as if anyone could possibly go back to sleep now. "We don't want to talk about it, man. We're all better off pretending nothing weird happened."

Thank goodness for Rafael.

Adelita frowns at the three of us. "Um, I'm not sure how healthy that is, or how long it'll last. Besides, I have questions aplenty." But when she drinks in the steely look on Cruz's face, she clams up. It's clear this isn't the time, and Cruz isn't the person to ask about La Sayona.

Cruz grabs his phone, sitting in the chair nearest the door while he pretends whatever is on his screen is terribly fascinating. When my eyes meet his embarrassed gaze, he looks away and makes a phone call instead of barking at Adelita, which I guess is a good thing.

I use the bathroom, in part, to grant myself a break from the tension in the room.

The sound of Cruz grumbling into his phone when I come back out cools the turmoil that's steadily been bubbling in the room since he woke. "We're on it. I get that you want us there now, but there's no way other than driving, and we're still a day or so away. What's this threat you're so worried about?" His disgusted sigh distracts us from the rough start to the morning. "Are you serious? That's it? That's all you're basing this on?" His attitude swings free sometimes, but he's quick to tether it back into place. "Yes, sir. We'll go check it out." He ends the call and starts another without looking up. "Hey, Dad. Can you have Aarón make up a room at home for the person we rescued?"

I note Cruz's cool avoidance of mentioning that the rescue is a woman. It means something, but I'm not sure what.

I'm grateful he's protecting Adelita, putting her up in his house.

Our house.

Adelita will be living with us.

A smile sweeps across my face in time with a frown taking over hers. "What's wrong?" I mouth as I stand before her. She's in the middle of the room looking so lost; I just have to be near her.

She doesn't just look sad, but suddenly worried. "I don't know Cruz. I don't want to live with a man who hurts me to get what he wants. Is there nowhere else I can stay?"

There are no blankets to hide us when my hand reaches out to twine my fingers through hers.

Rafael was pulling his shirt on, but he freezes at the sight, a giddy grin on his face.

I wait until she relaxes into the touch before I use my free hand to sign, tapping my chest. *I live with Cruz. You'll be living with me, if that's alright.*

This seems to lift her features from devastation to curiosity. "Say it again?"

I sign slower this time, loving the way her eyes track my movements.

She doesn't answer. Instead she closes the small gap between us and rests her forehead to my shoulder. She seeks me out for comfort, for safety when the world tilts uncertainly. It's the best feeling in the world.

I cup the back of her head, indulging in the softness of her raven waves. I've never cared much about hair, but now that she's letting me touch the strands, I decide on the spot that I only prefer this exact shade of black.

When Cruz ends the call and stands, that's the cue for all of us to get moving. I sit Adelita on the edge of the bed and gather up clean clothes for her, making sure she doesn't jostle her shoulder too much. The less it moves, the faster it will heal.

Cruz is usually all about business when it's time to go, but even after I finish with Adelita's shoulder, the bags are still only partially packed.

Cruz is seated across from Adelita on the other bed, his hand perpendicular to the floor to punctuate his edict. It's how he gets when he has to lay down the law without wanting to cause a scene about it.

"The Cáceres village is the safest place for you. We have a wall—a giant border wall surrounding our tribe. It keeps everyone else out. Even people who come from other tribes seeking asylum can't get in. It's totally safe."

Her nose crinkles. "You have a wall to keep the world out? Even people you are not at war with? How is that healthy? How can your village possibly evolve and thrive with no input or connections to the outside world?"

Cruz looks stumped, frowning with his eyebrows pushed together. Instead of answering, he sidesteps the question entirely. "You'll stay with me in my home because you don't know enough about the village or the Kalku to know when you're in danger. You have exactly one weapon to fight with: strength. If that's compromised, you're wide open to their attack. You need to be trained, but I don't want your ability made public. I'm guessing by the way you hid your secret from us for so long, you don't want people to know how strong you are either." Cruz purses his lips before continuing. "Somehow the Kalku know. That must be why they want you. If they are trying to capture you, then they have big plans for your ability. Best learn to hone them somewhere safe, so you can protect yourself."

She shakes her head, her entire demeanor downcast. She's got her free hand sandwiched between her knees. Her body is too tense. It's clear she doesn't trust Cruz.

"No. I won't go to the village with you. As much as I..." She clams up and then exhales. "No. Just no. I'll go to the curse tree with you, but after that, I'm out."

All sensation drains from my face. It can't be over this quickly.

"The village is the only place you'll be safe," Cruz counters.

"But I'm not safe with you. Taking me to the village where you can torture me however you wish? No, thanks."

Rafi holds up his hand. "For now, we don't have to talk about it. We know our next destination, which is the curse tree. All other talk can wait."

My doom is on the horizon. I need to make the most of the time we have together before she leaves us for good.

The Kalku will hunt her down. They've come for her twice now. They only do that if they're determined to see a capture through to the end, no matter what. Usually they'll move on to another victim.

I cannot let her part from us. She will be murdered, for certain.

"Santos, Rafi and I can train you on the way." Cruz rubs the nape of his neck, and I can tell that he's nervous. Sure, he's got bags under his eyes and he could use a shave—those things are standard for Cruz—but there's a hesitance to him now that's unfamiliar. "I've never invited a woman to live in my home before. Guess it played out about as well as I thought it would."

She nods once, but it's going to be a long road before he's earned her trust.

Cruz liberated me. He earned more than just my trust. He holds my unswerving loyalty. Without him and Rafael, I'd still be stuck in the cave, slave of the Kalku.

"I won't live with you," she rules in a quiet voice. "I don't know you. And what I do know scares me."

"That's fair." Cruz absorbs her honesty without brushing it aside. "How about I stay away from you as much as I can until you trust me?"

It's a kind offer, and not one Rafael or I expect him to give. He's usually not willing to bend on anything. His job isn't to understand nuances of emotion; he's the military's top warrior.

It's her quiet demeanor that forces him to lower his own volume, sanding off the edge in her tone to offer up something softer.

"Okay. That might be best."

Rafael starts to pack up his bag, and I realize I've been slacking. I elbow him out of the way and finish the job, securing Cruz's possessions and slinging his bag, Rafael's and mine over my shoulder, along with Adelita's things, which I put in the backpack I bought her last night.

"Is that mine?" she asks quietly. Everything she does is so soft, until it all explodes out of her, like when she murdered her attackers.

I nod, trying to explain why a purse isn't as easy to carry when you're on the road, and possibly on the run. It's black, like the rest of ours, but hers is brand new, and doesn't have the wear and tear ours do from years of combat and near-misses. Her purse is inside, along with toiletries and a change of clothes.

My new goal is to make sure Adelita doesn't experience any of the rougher life we're accustomed to. I want her backpack to stay untarnished.

We've added a fourth to our closed-off group.

"I can carry it, Santos. You're not a pack mule."

Rafael coils his arm around her waist and smooches her cheek. He's so casual with women on the road. Goodness knows the women in the village won't go near him. He fits in more gracefully out in the world like this. It's natural when he drapes his arm over any of them, so natural, in fact, that Adelita doesn't protest.

I try to picture myself doing something like that, but I'm

sure I'd do it wrong. Just holding her hand is a big deal for me.

Rafael doles out affections like that as if they're pocket treats for children. "Santos likes to make sure everything is taken care of. You sleep well, *linda?*"

"I did. Santos, honestly. You're carrying four backpacks. At least give me mine."

Rafael arrests his backpack from me and hands Cruz his. "Looks like the glory days of letting Santos carry our stuff is over."

I reluctantly hand over her pack, feeling lost without my role clearly defined. I'm to look after them. I'm to make sure they aren't bothered by anything. Now they're carrying their own bags? I'm unsure what to do with this as we walk out into the morning fog.

Rafael bats at the dense air, as if that will make him see better. "You in a funk this morning, Chief? Because this is overkill. It's too late in the morning for this much fog."

Cruz doesn't offer more than a grunt, which means he's preoccupied. The weather is definitely bowing to him, as it does when he isn't calm. I haven't felt the heat from the unfettered sun in a long time.

Adelita's wearing her pack on her good shoulder only. She tugs her long hair from under the strap, frowning at the inconvenience as we pile into the car.

Rafael is rattling off a list of all the things he can't wait to show Adelita when we get back to the village, but I'm not paying attention. Cruz pulls out of the parking lot and I motion for Adelita to turn her back to me.

It's far easier to braid her hair than it was Father's or any of the warriors'. They rarely washed it and never brushed. Adelita's hair is thick, long, silky, and is clearly bothering her, down as it is. I get a few inches in before she turns her chin, pausing my progress. "Are you… Are you braiding my hair?"

Rafael explains it all for me. "Back when he lived with the Kalku, one of his jobs was to get the warriors ready for battle. They all have long hair, which Santos, Santiago and the rest of the slaves braided for them."

"Oh. Well, thank you. I'm no good at putting my hair back with one hand, and it's been bugging me."

I smile and nod once, as if to tell her it's no trouble.

Then she says, "Can you sign all the things Rafael just said? If you don't, I'm never going to learn."

My heart swells in my chest that she wants to know how to communicate with me. I love that she's taking this step. I wish she didn't have to, of course, but curses are final, no matter how optimistic Cruz is that one day we'll find a cure for my muteness.

I indulge her, moving my fingers slowly so she can track which words mean what. Then I turn her head so I can finish braiding her hair. It's two braids that start above the far ends of her eyebrows and go back to the tips. Then I cross the ends and braid those into the sides of her head so there aren't any loose ends to bother her.

When she turns to face me, she's utterly angelic. The Kalku had ratty wisps that stuck out and made them look unhinged. She looks barely older than a teenager, ready to face the world with a beaming smile.

I love the look of happiness on her. I can see more of her face like this, which is just about the best sight in the world.

"Thank you. That's so much better."

Then instead of sliding back to the left side of the backseat, she takes the middle seat. My arm knows what to do on instinct, and wraps itself behind her so my fingers can play with the small curls at the base of her neck.

This, apparently, is the right thing to do. Adelita slumps as if she's gone suddenly boneless, and rests her temple to my shoulder. Her jugular is exposed, which is a clear display of trust.

She trusts me. Santos the Savage who was plucked from the Kalku and forced civilized people to coexist with him. Santos the Savage who makes women cringe with his scarred face and reputation for dining on the hearts of women.

My eyes sweep to the pulse thumping at her throat. The Kalku won't have her heart for their rituals. As long as I live, it'll stay safe inside of her. I find I'm protective of that thrum, that poetically steady drip of sanity that's strong enough to grant serenity to even us lowly savages.

I'm deliriously happy that I get to brush my fingers down her cheek. Her lashes shut out Rafael's giddy astonishment as he turns to give me an emphatic thumbs-up.

I hope the drive takes whole days, so I can stay just like this with her for as long as fate will allow.

20

COURAGE, BROTHER

CRUZ

"Why are we pulling over? The curse tree isn't for another couple hours." Rafael's been drumming on his knee for the past hour, and my nerves are just about shot from his constant movement.

I take the keys out of the ignition and pocket them, rousing Adelita and Santos from their couplish haze.

This isn't going to go over well but it's got to be done. "Santos, stay in the car. Adelita, come with me."

Santos never says no to me. I'm not sure he knows how. But the clear distress on his suddenly alert features tells me he's on the verge.

"Why can't Santos come?" she asks. I can hear the fear in her voice at being alone with me.

I certainly can't blame her for that. Maybe I shouldn't have hurt her to get the truth out of her.

Okay, the "maybe" part of that is clearly the thing I need to stop saying. I definitely shouldn't have hurt her.

But that's neither here nor there at this point. This arrangement is never going to work if she can't fall in line.

"Because Santos will get all bent out of shape if you break

a nail." When this answer doesn't suffice, I turn to face them all, even Rafi, who doesn't usually question me when I look as stern as I do now. "I'm guessing you don't have a lot of training in hand-to-hand combat. The Kalku know you're strong. Eventually, they'll have measures to counter that. You need to learn how to fight with more than just your strength."

She doesn't argue with my logic, but I can tell she doesn't like this one bit. "That sounds okay. How's Rafael at this kind of thing?"

"Rafi can get out of just about any tough spot. He's more agile than most."

"Then Rafi can train me, if he doesn't mind. Not to be difficult, but you've got a bee up your butt about me holding your hand last night, and I don't want you to take it out on my shoulder."

Rafael hangs his head as if he's just been sentenced. "Alright, *linda*. We can do that. I'm guessing that's why we're pulled over next to this bridge in the middle of Nowheresville?"

I nod toward the rural area. The greenery is cluttered with an unhealthy amount of weeds, and there's a dank stench to the concrete that make me wonder if the overpass is structurally sound.

I motion to the bridge, wincing at the phallic graffiti, which is next to some random names and expletives spray painted in huge letters.

Rafi doesn't giggle at the giant penis, so I know he's anxious about Adelita learning to defend herself.

I clear my throat. "This should give us enough cover to teach her the basics."

Rafael stretches and opens Santos' door. "Santos, you need to be trained as much as she does with this stuff." When Santos casts Rafi a soundless scoff of disbelief, Rafi clarifies.

"Not to teach you how to get out of Kalku attacks, but how not to lose your head when she's in trouble. Give Cruz your weapons and come with us."

We're all standing outside the car now, and I know the guys blame me for it being foggy and cold.

Santos turns his back to me so he can sign in angry bursts to Rafi, who takes it all in stride.

"Of course not. I won't hurt her shoulder. No, Santos. I won't hurt her at all. Just teaching her how to get out of holds and whatnot. Basic stuff. Very basic."

Santos doesn't look at me as he turns and hands me three knives, and then makes to return to Adelita's side. "All of them, Santos." I don't like laying down the law with him, but I also don't like that he's trying to get away with disobedience.

His head lowers like a scolded dog, and he slides the fourth knife out from his boot.

Adelita's upper lip curls in disgust that Santos feels compelled to obey me, but she doesn't understand. If I leave Santos with any sort of weapon, he'll hurt himself if he feels too much trauma. Watching Adelita get knocked around by Rafi will be too much for him, and I don't want him to harm himself again.

Santos hands over the fourth blade, and then lets me wrap my arms around him. I cup the back of his head and kiss his temple, hoping that shows him I want what's best for him, which is for Adelita to stay alive. Relying on brute strength, even at her caliber, is dangerous. It's understanding only one weapon, when there are hundreds that might come at you.

The tribe doesn't understand Santos. They think he's wild and sharpens his teeth with his knives. Really, he's a wounded pup who needs to be shown some patience while he figures out how to exist in the world that's made no room for someone like him. "Courage, brother. If you care about her safety, this needs to happen."

Santos grips my biceps to let me know he's filled with angst over this. Man, did he attach hard. He's seen bad things happen to loads of people, but he always shakes it off without a blink, immune to almost everything. But this woman stumbles into our lives, and he's smitten worse than anyone I've ever seen.

I feel Adelita's eyes on us, measuring our embrace. "I can't tell if you're cruel or sweet," she comments when I meet her gaze. "I don't get to see many men hug as often as you all do. It's nice."

"I'm cruel," I tell her, leaving no room for any sort of softness to enter her perception of me. "They're sweet. We meet halfway."

Rafi kisses her temple. "Men in the village don't have as many insecurities about masculinity. We're defending our village every day by hunting down the Kalku, so there's no need to pretend hugs make a man weak."

Adelita wraps her arm around Rafi's middle, squeezing him because it's clear she likes the idea of our dynamic. "I wish more of my patients could open up like that."

I'm hardly the pillar for a well-adjusted man, but whatever settles that spooked look in her eyes at the prospect of being near me is a good thing in my book.

When we make our way under the grubby overpass, I stick close to Santos while Rafi holds Adelita's hand. Though I know I'm right, I'm also positive I'm going to regret all of this.

MY HEART
RAFAEL

I hate this whole thing. It's not enough to play the part of the total tool who would abduct a woman, but doing it all while Santos' face whines like a wounded animal is more than I can bear. "Santos, honestly. I'm not hurting her. Tell him, *linda*."

She dons a reassuring smile that's too filled with nerves to be believable. "Nothing hurts, Santos. It's more annoying than anything else. I promise I'll get good at this. Then you'll never have to see it again."

If only that was true. I coil my forearm around her neck, careful not to clamp down on her windpipe. I'm doing her a disservice, really. The Kalku grip you and pinch your throat when they get you from behind. They hold your scream as if they want to collect it and take it home with them. Even like this, she's reluctant to put any real force behind the escape maneuver for this hold. Not that I don't appreciate her restraint so I don't get hurt, but we're not going to get anywhere playing it safe like this.

Instead of physical harm, I draw her spine to my chest so I can whisper enough to properly motivate her. "It will not be me coming for you; it will be men who know nothing of how to be kind. They want you for your strength, but you don't understand what they'll do with it. They don't want to put you to work." I jerk her backward, taking a few steps so she's off-balance.

It takes far too long for her to regain her footing. That's one lesson failed.

"What do they want?" She speaks in a meek tone that suggests she wouldn't have it in her to harm a fly.

Lesson two is failed because a handful of seconds is all it takes for the Kalku to tear out the voice box of a screaming woman.

I keep quiet because I'm ashamed. I don't want to scare Adelita. She's been nothing but nice to me, tolerant of Cruz, and an angel to Santos. But the urgency to escape isn't there, so I have to find a new way to motivate her.

"They believe a man can steal elongated life through eating the hearts of women. Virgins are their specialty. Purer lifeforce or something."

"But I'm not..." she trails off, and I can feel her skin heating with chagrin.

I can't help my chuckle. "They also believe a man can gain superior abilities and awareness by eating the heart of his victim. If they want to gain better eyesight, they'll abduct a woman with superior sight, cut out her heart, boil it down and drink the stew. If I had to put my money on it, that's why they want you. They want your strength."

"What? That's awful! Are you serious?"

I jerk my forearm to let her know this is no joke. "They'll come at you from all angles because they don't take chances in securing the hearts they want. The one who grabs you from behind will tear out your voice box. They're firm believers in silencing their prey." I don't stop for her gasp, but press deeper into the horror. "Once you're surrounded, they bind you and take you to the cave. You're not allowed to speak to the men." My breath is heavy in her ear, and I know I'm scaring her.

I hate it, but I know it's what must be done. I need her to fight back, or Santos will lose the only woman who's ever looked at him like he's a man.

I grip her tighter. "In every cave, there's a deep pit they've carved out. That's where they take the women and dump them while they prepare."

Now she's squirming. "Stop it! Rafael, tell me you're lying."

"They want you afraid, so they'll spend days keeping you in the dark where no one can find you."

I'm speaking quietly, but Santos picks out my threats easily. *"Three days in the pit,"* he mouths, holding up three fingers. I can tell he's picturing her there, judging by the sickened look on his face.

I hold Adelita tighter, keeping the restraint so intrusive that she'll need to struggle out of it soon. "They want your heart at its most active, pumping terror through you so when they cut it out of your chest, it's ripe and ready for them."

Her chest is heaving with anxiety, and I hate it. How those sick bastards get off on terrorizing women is beyond me.

"Your fear makes them stronger, bolder. So no matter what, you cannot give it over to them."

I can feel her hard swallow before she nods. "So what do I do?"

"Guard your throat. Work your hand up between your neck and my arm and shove it off of you."

She does as I ask, and looks so proud of herself, I almost want to call it a day.

"Alright. Again." Only this time, I pin her free arm behind her back.

She struggles and then harrumphs. "Well, I can't. I need my arm free."

"You don't have it free. Pop out your backside so I'm lifted off my feet. Then you can flip me over your top half."

Santos trots over to us and removes my arm from her, taking her place as my captive. He holds his hands behind his back to demonstrate what she should do.

I don't look forward to being thrown to the ground by an emotionally taxed Santos, but I guess that's the job today.

Screw you, Cruz. I don't want to be the one coaching her through this.

The second I've got my hand on Santos' throat, he pops my pelvis with his backside, flips me overtop his body and then presses his boot to my throat. He mimes stomping on my nose to incapacitate me, and for the life of me, I'm not sure how I ended up being the tackling dummy for Santos.

We do the maneuver several times before he lets her try it again.

She gets me over her good shoulder, but she's scared to hurt me, so the whole move isn't truly effective. She practically cradles me to the ground, she's so sweet.

"Did I hurt you?" she frets, her eyebrows tented with true worry.

I let out a dramatic groan to get her to lean nearer. As soon as she's on her knees next to me, whimpering with worry, I prop myself up on my elbows and kiss her cheek.

Her neck shrinks and a girlish smile takes over her face. It's so cute, I truly hope Cruz calls it a day so we can leave it all at that.

But of course, I'm not that lucky.

It's a long afternoon spent with me being gently folded over people's shoulders before until Cruz finally intervenes. "Rafi, take Santos for a walk. I need a word with Adelita."

Sure, give me the impossible job. "You alright with that, *viento?*"

Adelita looks uncomfortable, but nods. "It's fine."

I take her at her word, though I'm not sure that's wise. "Come on, Santos. I saw a sign for a gas station up there. Cruz, you've got the time it takes us to refuel. Best I can do."

Cruz nods but Santos' terror is plain. It's hard to watch Santos go from displaying unswerving loyalty for Cruz to this. It's not defiance, it's obedience that crushes parts of his soul, which feels so much worse than actual insolence. I don't want to teach him this lesson—to walk away from someone he loves when she's about to undergo something big.

Maybe it's too soon for him to love her, but that doesn't stop it from being true.

Santos takes one step away from her, and it's too much. He drops down to his knees before Cruz, doubling over and lacing his hands over the nape of his neck. It's the position the Kalku force their captives to take when they've surrendered.

Though Cruz pretends he doesn't see it, I know he's not dense. Santos is surrendering because he feels he's the captive once again. Cruz is his master, and he feels powerless to breathe the air of the freedom we promised him.

Adelita understands only the basics: Santos is distraught because he doesn't want to leave her with Cruz.

I glower at Cruz, who pretends he doesn't see me. There's a lot he pretends he doesn't see.

Adelita lowers herself to sit on her heels next to Santos. Her hand rests on his twined fingers, and just like that, his arms go limp at his sides. "It's alright." She traces her fingers down his nape, doing what she can to soothe his angst. "I'm not helpless, Santos. I just didn't want to accidentally hurt Rafael, so I was going easy on him." Her eyes dart up to our fearless leader, still sizing up the stern angle of his jaw. "I don't have those same hang-ups about Cruz."

She guides Santos' head to rest on her lap, and it's just about the strangest thing I've ever seen. I remember how Santos was when we found him—filthy and wearing only shorts. Long hair, knotted and ratty. Afraid of nothing but direct sunlight. Now he's a puppy for her, childlike and innocent.

I don't tell her that the slaves were also given the heart broth to drink. I don't mention anything about his former life that she doesn't need to know. I wouldn't dream of doing anything that might stop her from looking at him lovingly, like how she does while she runs her fingers through his hair.

The air feels still and sacred as her sweetness permeates the outdoors. "It's alright, my heart."

Santos sags against her as if she's taken all the tension from his body.

My heart. The man the tribe was convinced didn't deserve a voice earns the nickname "my heart." It's so stinking adorable, I can hardly stand it. But I do. I stand there and watch with rapt fascination, transfixed at what a little tenderness can do to a savage.

If her limit is that she can only be as strong as she is gentle, then I know for a fact that I'm looking at the strongest person in the world.

"Go with Rafael," she insists. "I'll be okay."

I glower at Cruz for creating a team dynamic where one of us has to say those words.

Santos has been through enough.

But Cruz is ever our vigilant leader, and disagrees.

My heart thunders as I help Santos to his feet and lead him away, regretting every step that takes him away from Adelita.

22

WORSE THAN DEATH
CRUZ

I wait until the car pulls away before I roll my shoulders. For crying out loud, that was dramatic. "Alright, that's good. I need you to trust me if this is ever going to work."

She quirks her eyebrow at me. "I don't trust you. I just know you won't stop until you get your way. At least this time you're sparing Santos having to watch. So go ahead. What information do you need this time?"

I balk at her moxie. She's such a kitten around Santos but she's a pit bull with me. "You were holding back with Rafi. That's not going to help Santos when a real attack comes."

That's all the warning I give her.

She's one-armed right now, so I'm not expecting her to truly be able to defend herself properly. However, excuses aren't tolerated during actual combat, so when I charge at her and she doesn't move in time, I knock her flat on her back.

She lays there, blinking up at the underside of the manky bridge in stunned silence.

"Up!" I bellow. "You would be dead right now if this was a real attack. You've got strength. Use it!"

It's tedious to watch her struggle to stand. A bleat of agony escapes her lips when she moves her shoulder too far. She's got only the one hand with which to balance herself. But I have to remind myself that helping her now will only hurt her in the long run.

Once she's on her feet, I charge again. This time, she's smart enough to sidestep me, her hand catching my shoulder and delivering a shove so hard, my feet leave the ground.

As I hit the dirt, I'm relieved. "That's perfect," I tell her, righting myself with a grimace. "That's what I wanted to know. I need you to do that again, but harder. Can you hit harder?"

Adelita smirks at me, as if I've just given her a grand present. "I can try."

"Good." I can't help the relief that curves my lips into half a smile. "This is our language, then. I had to find one for Santos, and now this is ours. I piss you off, and you beat the crap out of me."

"I like everything about that." Her words are cocky but it's clear she's still scared to hurt me.

I go back to my starting point and slap the back of my shoulder. "Aim here next time, though. Knocking me sideways off my path won't get you as much mileage as shoving me forward so my face hits the ground."

I've angered her enough since we met that she won't hold back this time.

I hope.

Jeez, she's strong.

When I charge her this time, she sidesteps me and shoves where I instructed, but she leaves her leg in the way to give me something to trip over. I'm airborne from her shove and well-timed trip. When my back hits the ground after doing an unintentional flip, I'm impressed and not bothered in the least that she's knocked the wind out of me.

I expect her to let me get myself up without assistance, but I don't expect her to stand over me with her shoe atop my chest to pin me in place. "You and I are going to talk about this. Hurting me back at that first motel to force information out of me was wrong. Until you admit that, we won't move past it."

"You forget that I don't care if we're past it or not."

"I wouldn't care either if Santos wasn't in the picture, but he is. He loves you, so somehow, we need to find a way to get along. That means no more torturing me. If you need information you think I have, well that's just too bad." Her mouth is firm and she points down at my chest with authority. It's clear she's not used to asserting herself. Insecurity runs rampant in her eyes even as she tries to be intimidating. "And one day soon, we're going to talk about La Sayona. You all acted like you expected some ghost woman to come at me with a knife or something."

I scowl up at her. I don't like to make a habit of apologizing, and I'm not about to start the useless ritual now.

Instead, I reach up and move her flimsy shoe from my chest up to my throat. "Here. This is the vulnerable spot. If you're here, I can just..." I move her foot back to where it was and cuff her ankle, locking my elbow and rolling over onto my side away from her, taking her leg with me.

Her shriek is so squeaky and mouse-like as she topples over my body that I can't help but chuckle.

She's a pile of limbs atop my side, but she doesn't look hurt, only shocked. Her mouth is open as she twists away and sits up.

"What? Did you want me to go easy on you?"

"It's not that." She points at my face once I slide out from beneath her. "You have dimples."

My mouth goes immediately taut, erasing all signs of my laughter. Is that a compliment? Why? What use is a compliment on someone like me? What sort of game is she playing? "Whatever. Let's go again. This time, make sure your foot stays on my throat."

She shakes her head as if I've said something foolish. "I mean, what a total waste. Dimples on a man who never smiles."

"Shut it."

"Or maybe you just don't smile when you're on the road. How many days a year exactly might that be?" When I don't answer as I stand, she seems to take that as some sort of nonverbal response. "You wouldn't be trapping yourself into a life that ensures you never smile, would you? I can't imagine what the purpose of that would be."

Just for that, I don't bother helping her up. I point my finger at her across the divide of the hard ground between us. "Stop trying to get into my head. You're a shrink, and I know your tricks."

"Oh, you do?" She brushes off her jeans with one hand. "So you've been to therapy before? How long ago was that?"

I blanch. "I've never been to a therapist, thank you very much."

She feigns shock, her hand going to her chest. "No! You seem so well-adjusted. Why, any time I want to talk to someone, my natural inclination is also to hurt them where they've just been stabbed. Because I'm well-adjusted and clever, like you."

I'm done waiting. I charge at her out of sheer frustration this time, not letting her sidestep me quite so easily. I check her with my hip and send her flying like a ragdoll. Her body skips twice before she lands with a wince.

I know I've hurt her, but that's not the main takeaway. She needs to understand why we're doing this or it's going to crush her, which isn't what I want. I want her stronger. I want her to be able to stand on her own against the Kalku, though I can't imagine the guys or I would ever leave her to fight them alone.

But her bitten-off scream over her injured shoulder hitting the ground far too hard tears me up more than I'd like to admit.

Maybe that was a bit too rough.

I trot over to her and again refuse to give her a hand up. In my experience, people get too many of those. It makes the world weak, and that's not a thing I'll tolerate on my crew. She's still on her back, too stunned to stand.

I try not to snarl at her, but keep my voice low and even. In control.

That's right, therapist. You're not getting under my skin at all.

"As much as you probably think I don't care, I do. I care about Santos. If you're taken, he won't be able to handle it. He can barely handle going to the gas station if he thinks you're in fake danger. And I care that Rafi has someone who looks at him the way you do. I care that the Kalku don't get what they want, which is you." I press my boot to her throat, which is so dainty, I could probably crush it without much effort.

Her growl finds me through her pain. "Get off me."

"Make me," I order her without removing my foot.

I watch the steps of what I just did to upend her flicker over her mind and come up to a barrier. "I can't roll over like you did, or I'll hurt my shoulder."

I shrug. "You should probably explain it to the Kalku just like that. I'm sure they'll back off and hand you some roses to help you feel better." I give my boot a little more weight. "If you want to live through all of this, you're going to get hurt. Santos will baby you, but I won't. I want you to live, which it doesn't sound like you've done a whole lot of, Miss Erased in

Five Minutes. If you want to get up, if you want a life, if you want to live, you have to fight for it. Make me move, Adelita!"

Anger wells up in her and I know I've touched on something crucial. She's livid that I'm right, but it's just enough to give her the bravery to cuff my ankle and roll her body onto her bum shoulder. She lets out a shriek of agony that almost sounds like triumph as she takes my body with her, toppling me ungracefully. My knee smacks hard on the ground, however I feel nothing but proud of her effort.

I worry that my shin might be too heavy to rest on her as I palm the ground. She's curvy but delicate at the same time.

The noise that belts from her sounds like a declaration, like she won't let herself be quiet anymore. It's rough and raw and real, and I love it.

My chest heaves as I grip the grass. "That's good. Real good. Keep hold of my ankle. You fought for my leg, and you've got it. Don't let go. Twist it up until something breaks. Try to touch my ankle to the back of my thigh."

If this were a real fight, she'd be moving much too slow, but that doesn't matter right now. We're practicing.

She manages to bend my leg until my knee smarts. "Like that?"

I don't want her snatched at. She makes Santos happy.

She notices if I smile.

"That's great, Addy." I grimace that I've given her a nickname. Hopefully she doesn't notice. "Once you've got him like this, jerk his leg outward in a sharp tug, and don't stop until he's crying because you've broken something important. Then he can't run after you. If you fight anyone from the Kalku, the objective is to always make it the last time that person can come after you."

She releases my leg but I don't get up. "Did I hurt you?"

"Nah."

But her dainty hand finds its way to my calf muscle and

starts rubbing. "I did. You hit the ground too hard. I wasn't careful. I'm sorry, Cruz."

That's the real move for incapacitation. It's not violence; it's tenderness that does me in. My whole body slumps on the grass. I know I should jerk away from the light massage, but dang, it's been ages since a woman's touched me like that.

My mouth goes slack and I wonder if I have the brain cells to care if I start drooling right now.

Finally the fog around us clears and the clouds go away. It's the first time sun has kissed my skin in... I can't remember the last time I was in direct sunlight.

"You did well," I offer her. "It takes warriors a while to get over the pain thing. Most think pain is the worst thing that can happen to them, but they're always wrong."

"Death," she rasps, and I can tell her shoulder is still on fire. "Death is the worst."

A guttural groan escapes me as she drains the tension from my calf. "Wrong again. Capture is worst. Once the Kalku get their hands on you, you'll wish for the mercy of a quick death. Keep that in mind when you worry about being in pain."

When she nods, by some miracle, I manage to inch away from the tenderness and slap life back into my cheeks to regain my stoic demeanor. Softness does no one a lick of good on the road.

It takes some effort, but I finally bring myself to stand. "Alright. Let's do that again."

23

CRUZ'S LESSONS
ADELITA

It's five more times of the stupid ankle cuff move before Santos and Rafael return with the car.

My shoulder hurts so bad that I'm soaked in sweat. My hands are shaking and my shoulder has long since grown tired of screaming at me to stop, stop, please stop.

But even as the guys come down the hill toward us, I know I have to finish the choreography or Cruz will throw a fit. He holds his hand up to keep Santos from interfering, but I know that won't last forever.

I cuff Cruz's ankle again and roll onto my side, shrieking through the pain that means nothing, will stop nothing. I keep rolling until I'm on my stomach, and then on my other side, and then facing the underside of the bridge. Through it all I don't let go of Cruz's leg, but keep it as my trophy for a job well done.

Finally, I did it right.

Cruz is flat on his stomach, giving me a muffled thumbs-up that I didn't let go of his ankle at all this time.

The pain is so bad, I'm certain my hearing has been affected. Rafael is yelling something, but I don't absorb it.

I sit up on my own, because that's what warriors do.

I did it. I did the thing I try to get my patients to do. It took some pain, but I finally found my voice. That part of me that goes quiet when it should shout cracked the air when I took Cruz down. I can feel myself changing on the inside, declaring that yes, I am a person, and I'm allowed to take up some space in this universe.

I have a voice, and for the first time, I'm not afraid of it.

My body is quivering, not from fright, but from my shoulder going into some sort of agony overdrive. I'm hoping my faked smile will earn me some sort of "Wow! Adelita's amazing!" reaction from Santos.

Judging by the terror on his face as he runs to me, I'm guessing that's not going to happen.

Santos is beside himself as he drops to his knees and leans my temple to his chest. Relief floods through me simply because he's here. I know that's cheesy, and far too soon to feel things like this, but I can't help it. If Santos is here, the pain will stop. That's who he is to me. I don't feel that clawing ache from missing my mama. I don't worry that I'll always be alone.

His hands are quaking as they ghost over me, but mine are finally steadying as I lean into him.

My eyes close after he signs something to Rafi one-handed. My sling is removed, and my lashes pop back open when I feel Rafi's hands on my collar. I squeak when he rips my shirt open from collar to sleeve, exposing... "Is that blood? Am I bleeding?"

My stitches are ripped and fresh crimson is oozing out. My lower lip quivers, muffling my hiss as the dank under-bridge air hits my open wound.

"How did you not notice you were bleeding? How does one not feel stitches ripping open?" Rafi shouts more at Cruz than at me.

"I mean, it hurts, but I thought I was wet because I'm sweating. And the grass is a little dewy from the fog."

Santos lays me down while Cruz cusses and runs to get the healer bag from the car. He tosses it next to Santos, who wastes no time numbing my arm with some sort of serum shot. I'm too distracted by the pain to ask about it.

Cruz runs his fingers through his short hair. Somehow the look of worry on him makes me that much more aware of everything that hurts. Worry isn't his jam. Control is sacrosanct to him, so when he loses it, I know things must be dire.

My eyes flick to my doctor, whose lips are pursed in concentration. "Santos, I don't know about this. You didn't need that before. I'm probably okay."

"Santos wasn't nearly as smitten back then as he is now," Rafi explains. "Numbing your pain is more for him than it is for you. He can't stand the sight of you in agony." Rafael swipes at some sweat on my forehead with his thumb. "You hanging in there, *viento*? Can I get you anything?"

"I'm okay. I just… Whoa." A wave of something cold rolls through me. In the next breath, my shoulder doesn't hurt nearly as much. In fact, it doesn't bother me at all. Nothing bothers me anymore.

My legs go limp while Santos and Rafael tend to my injury. My head lolls to the side, and my eyes lock in on Cruz's, who's standing away from us, his lips stubbornly impassive while his eyes scream an apology.

I don't need it, though. In fact, I don't need anything. Everything that seemed so important mere minutes ago floats by on a sea of nothingness.

Santos signs something and Rafi's eyes widen. "We have to move her? Do you really think that's best?"

Because Santos is so worked up, I catch every word he

mouths while he signs. *"She bled on the ground. The Kalku will track her down. We have to go now!"*

Santos. So handsome. So good to me.

My mouth goes slack, and finally Cruz comes to life. "Adelita? Addy! Santos, you used too much sedative." He clears the distance between us and kneels above my head, tilting his face over mine while he says… something.

"Home," I manage to work out. I want to go home, back to my own bed.

Cruz's eyes steel with determination before he nods once. "Okay, Addy. I'll take you home, then. *My* home."

I open my mouth to protest, but I can't remember the right words. I don't want to go to the village. I already said as much.

Cruz goes over my head. "Santos is right. Your blood is all over the grass. If they want you as badly as I'm guessing, then they'll find you far easier than I'd like. The village can protect you." His eyes flicker with worry. "You'll be safe there. I promise, you'll be safe."

I don't believe him, but I appreciate the lie. He says something else, but I can't make it out.

I'm tired now, too tired to worry about the Kalku or my stitches. I give up the fight on trying to stay awake and let myself get pulled under into the cold nothing that greets me with open arms.

"She doesn't want to go to the village," Rafi reminds Cruz when my eyes close.

"That doesn't matter anymore," Cruz says in his typical tyrannical fashion. "She's one of us now, so she's ours to protect. The village is the safest place."

No. I don't want to go to the village. I don't want to live with Cruz. I don't want to reside in a place where they protect their delicate sensibilities with a great border wall. I told them as much already.

I don't belong with anyone who looks down on Santos, thinking he's savage.

When the guys don't say anything else, and I'm too tired to form words, Cruz continues. "It's the only option if we want Adelita to live through the relentless hounding from the Kalku. They will stop at nothing until they have her."

An ominous horror rings through my body at the grave reality of his words.

Worry weights my bones, but finally unconsciousness drags me under, reminding me that I cannot control my fate.

I have to trust them, whether I'm ready for that adventure or not.

Love the book? Leave a review!

...otherwise, I'll make sure Santos
eats Adelita's heart in book two.

You have been warned!

DANGEROUS HEARTS

Enjoy a free preview from *Dangerous Hearts*,
the second novel in the "Savage Hearts" series.

THINGS I CAN'T UNDO
CRUZ

My sister's greeting at our return to the tribe has been slightly lackluster. "You're an absolute idiot," Eva says, folding her arms with a frown.

I cast Eva a glower but she never cowers under the weight of my frustration. "Not helping." Normally everyone in the house finds an excuse to get away from me at the slightest sign of my temper, but Eva regards me as if I'm being annoying.

Only a sister can get away with that.

She taps her foot as she stares me down. "You tell father you're bringing home a rescue and that you're setting them up in our home. Quite the convenient omission of a pronoun. Then lo and behold, you come home with an actual woman, carrying her like she's a fainted bride over the threshold. Beautiful as the day is long. What did you expect?"

"Santos was shaking too badly to carry her and Rafi's pissed about something so I *had* to carry her."

Me. Rafi's pissed at me because I was too rough with Adelita when I tried to train her to stand up to the Kalku. Addy is the strongest person I've ever come across but learning how to be strategic and agile in your fighting is still a necessity when you're a beautiful woman with a target on your back.

But I leave all those details out so I don't have to soak in another layer of my sister's wrath. Eva's got a mouth on her when she gets worked up. Why can't she be wary of me, like everyone else in the village?

Eva starts pacing in front of the kitchen's long island. "Her. Her. Who is she? Does she have a name? Dad's already announced to the tribe that you've brought home a woman to live in your house. Do you know how that sounds?"

I hold back a groan of frustration. "It sounds like a marriage announcement he had no right making. He can have fun prying his foot from his mouth. I certainly didn't do anything to encourage this."

Eva glances up at the ceiling as if praying for patience. "It's like you want me to yell at you. Do you not understand how long the tribe has been waiting for you to choose a bride so you can continue the family line? Everyone assumed you'd..."

I know what she's going to say. She's not wrong. I'm supposed to end up alone. That's the point of La Sayona's curse.

I roll my shoulders and avoid Eva's needling. "How does me bringing home a random survivor equal out to a wedding?"

Her glare cuts to me, her hands on her hips. She's only an inch shorter than me, which is taller than most of the men in the village. She wears her height like it gives her an extra boost of authority, which I can't imagine she needs. She has sheer volume, birthright and tenacity on her side. The height is just overkill.

Arms akimbo, she lowers her voice to properly scold me. "It does when you're next in line to produce an heir the whole tribe is counting on. You know how the villagers feel about outsiders."

"I think the giant border wall around our tribe speaks for itself." I cannot believe I'm letting Eva bait me, but apparently, I can't help myself. Adelita's earlier criticism of our wall stuck in my brain. "I know the gig. We rescue victims from the Kalku. Sometimes we even let them into the village for our healers to get them back on their feet. Then we pat ourselves on the back for what compassionate heroes we are, but really everyone in Cáceres is counting the seconds until the newcomers are out of here. The second the outsiders enter the village, they're treated like lepers. Can't have the purity of the tribe infected by too many foreigners."

Eva rears back at my blunt assessment, but recovers coolly, as she always finds a way to do. "Survivors usually are sent to the healer's home, not the chief's home, and then they're placed outside of the village once they're recovered from whatever the Kalku put them through. They don't take up residence in the village, much less the chief's home."

"Santos did."

She narrows her eyes at me, her sarcasm flaring. "Yes. I'm sure if you married Santos, even that would be an improve-ment to your current state."

I grab an apple from the teal-painted pottery bowl in the center of the kitchen's island, rubbing it on my shirt before taking a bite. Man, I miss fresh food. Weeks of gas station grabs and takeout is the worst. "You're just mad because if I had brought home a wife, the heat would be off of you to find a husband."

She lets out a long exhale like she's purging the air from a tire. "That would be a bonus, yes. Dad set me up with another one of his selections while you were away. As if that's all it takes."

"Let me guess: A decorated warrior who hasn't cracked a smile since he was a toddler."

"It's almost like you've heard me complain about this before."

"One or two hundred times, yes."

The bickering cools between us, since we're in the same boat. She wants to continue to sit in on policy meetings with Dad, but if she gets married, that spot will go to her husband. Our tribe is a pretty strict patriarchy. I'm to rule next, and I couldn't want the job less.

She paces about the beige-tiled kitchen, her teal dress matching the countertops as she turns on her heel and marches back and forth. "I'm not sure how much clearer I can be that I have no desire to marry a warrior. My father is the chief who worked his way up from being a warrior himself. My uncle is head of the army. My brother is a highly revered warrior who is completely daft when it comes to women, and who, come to think of it, also hasn't cracked a smile since he was a toddler. I don't want that life. I want to affect change at the highest level."

"And if you ever did get married? If you could have both a position of prominence and a husband?"

Before she speaks, I already know what she's going to say. "I want a poet. I want to laugh and enjoy my marriage, like Mom and Dad do. I don't want to bite my nails for the rest of my life, adding a husband to the list of men I love who I'm constantly afraid might never come home every time they step foot outside this village."

She started out in her usual rant, but it ends on a pained note that hits me right between the ribs. "I missed you too, Eva."

She rolls her eyes at me, though I can see there are tears glistening. "Oh, you're impossible."

When Dad comes in with a grand, "So who's going to

introduce me to my future daughter-in-law?" I groan, and have to explain myself all over again.

It's hard to watch disappointment bloom on my father's face. I do all I can never to catch that look directed at me. I don't know how to avoid it today, though. He looks like me, only jolly and a good thirty pounds overweight. The only way I can picture myself joyful is to look at my father and take away a few years. He's got black hair that hasn't thinned or receded, no matter how much strain the tribe puts on us. He's thick chested, tall and with a stern jawline that I put to better use than he ever could.

Father rarely accesses his disapproval, but I can feel it through the veil of love he wears like a medal of honor.

I scratch the nape of my neck. "I can still introduce you to the newcomer, though. You might want to wait until she's awake. Conversation might be a bit one-sided if you go in now."

Dad recovers as best he can. "Well, I suppose that would be nice. Tell me about this woman."

I shrug. "Name's Adelita."

Addy. I called her "Addy" like she's my playground girlfriend or something. I'm glad she didn't highlight that slip up.

I lean against the counter. "Not much to tell. Actually, you should ask Santos all about her. He could tell you plenty."

Dad's face drains, reminding me that I'm terrible at jokes. "Tell me she wasn't abducted by the Kalku. Tell me you rescued her before they did their damage."

"Nothing like that. I just meant Santos has it bad for her, so he would know better about Adelita than I do."

Father and Eva both gape at me, stunned just as I had been at the prospect. I'm not sure if it was more unbelievable that Santos was capable of something as human as attraction, or if the real shocker was that a woman was showing interest in him.

I grimace at how mean my thoughts sound. Santos is awesome; it's just that the woman in the village are terrified of their resident savage. They don't do well with outsiders, especially ones who lived with the vicious Kalku.

My father doesn't completely regain his composure, but places his hands on the island as his usual smile takes over his features. "Well, that settles it. I must get to know her first thing. I heard her talking while I passed through the hallway."

"Then she's awake now. Knock yourself out."

"If she's awake, why are you out here? She's a rescue, which means you should be with her. Unless..." Eva sees through me, narrowing her eyes while I squirm. "You did something, didn't you."

Darn her for knowing too much when she couldn't possibly know anything about it. I don't want to admit to Eva that I pushed Addy too hard. I'm the one who tore her stitches—twice now. I didn't just toughen her up; I hurt her. Santos had to give her enough sedative for her to pass clean out.

Still, I hate it when Eva's right. She gloats, and I'm not in the mood for it today. "You don't know what you're talking about. I'm not avoiding anything."

She holds up her hands like only the most vexing little sisters can do. "I never said you were avoiding her. But while we're on the subject, why are you avoiding her?"

I run my tongue along the top row of my teeth before speaking. "If you think we're too old for me to throw you into the pond, you're wrong."

"Children," Dad scolds, but it's the most he cares to redirect us. It's all we need to fall in line.

I grab an apple for Adelita, guessing she's probably

hungry since she missed the last meal due to being, well, passed out. I lead them down the many winding corridors toward my room. It's just pragmatic that Adelita is set up in the bedroom next to mine. Santos and I hem her room in, so it's the safest place in the house.

I knock four times in a pattern the three of us know. *Rat rat-a-tat*, letting Santos know it's me.

He's not quick to answer the door. In fact, when it does swing open, it's Rafael. My oldest friend doesn't greet me, but kisses my father and sister on the cheek instead. "Come on in. Good to see you, Dad."

I wish Rafi could take the mantle of keeping the family name going, but the tribe was insistent: just because Dad adopted Rafael and Santos and made them my brothers doesn't mean they can rule. Their children won't be of the royal bloodline.

Shortsighted idiots.

"Good to see you too, Son. I hear we have a new guest in our home. Care to introduce me?" My dad's smile comes easily, though he keeps his voice quiet, as if Addy's a newborn or something.

Adelita. Not Addy.

Rafi gives Dad a sharp nod and a forced smile as he ushers them inside. This room was largely used as our hangout, but upon my call home, Dad and Aarón had the place outfitted with a canopy bed, white linens and gilded fixtures. It truly is a room for a future Tribeswoman.

It's the room that weights me with his silent disappointment more than anything else. I can see his high expectations for me, and how I've never fulfilled that one item on his checklist. He wants me happy, and thinks this is the way to get me there. He also wants me to secure our family's legacy, which is no small responsibility. It's also nearly impossible, given my nightly predicament.

Santos is sitting on the bed, his boots off and his back against the ornate headboard. I groan internally at the wood-carvings that look freshly done, and tell the story of our family's rise to power. Dad tends to go overboard when he's happy. This was meant for my future bride, which Adelita is not.

And there she is, wrapped in a white blanket, cradled on Santos' lap. She's small, all curled up against him with her head on his shoulder. Her nose is pink and her eyes are rimmed in red while Santos brushes his fingers over her raven braids. He's careful with her, like he's stroking glass. The strongest person I've ever met, and he's treating her like it matters when a person breaks.

Adelita will soon learn that it doesn't, and she'll be stronger for it.

"This is our new friend?" Dad asks Santos, sitting gingerly on the edge of the bed. His voice is quiet to match the hushed mood.

Santos nods but doesn't get up to bow and kiss the floor, as he always does when Dad enters the room. Dad's told him a million times that it's not necessary, but it's the only thing Santos has ever been obstinately disobedient about. He reveres the man who welcomed him into his home after he was rescued from the Kalku. Santos adores the father who regards him as a man and not a slave.

Instead of the usual bowing, he holds Adelita tight. It's like he's afraid that if he lets go, she'll come to ruin. In our home. Where there's never been an attack from the Kalku. The other two tribes never bring their turf wars onto our soil, either. Our village is the safest in the world but Santos' hackles are still raised. He coils his arms tighter around her ribs to guard her, even from our dad.

If that's what it's like to be in love, I don't want anything to do with it. I can't imagine feeling the protectiveness I do for my people along with this overwhelming need to make sure a fully capable woman doesn't get her feelings hurt or some nonsense.

I don't want anything like that for myself, but for some reason, I can't look away.

It's an obvious effort for Santos to pry one hand away from her body, but he does so to sign to my father a few details about the woman in his arms. *"This is Adelita. The Kalku want her."* Then he strokes Addy's braids so lovingly, Eva coos, her hand moving over her heart. *"We belong to each other."*

It's the strangest and the most perfect thing I never expected Santos to say. I don't even know if Adelita agrees with it because she can't speak sign. By the way she's molded her body to his, I'm guessing she doesn't have any real reservations about the intensity of their connection.

Dad is careful with his volume and chooses his words slowly. "It's nice to meet you, Adelita. Where are you from?"

She answers, and Dad goes through the litany of questions we always ask when someone's had a run-in with the Kalku.

True to form, Adelita doesn't respond when Dad asks why the Kalku were targeting her. When he looks to me for the truth, I cross my arms over my chest and give him a firm shake of my head. I don't often keep secrets from my dad, but this one doesn't belong to me. It's hers, and I've forced her into too much as it is. I have faith that she'll trust Dad with the truth in time, after he's proven his character enough for her liking.

Besides, the less people know about her ability, the better. If Tio Bruno finds out, he'll draft her into the band of warriors first thing, which would be an utter disaster. She's too gentle for anything like that. Too afraid of herself. I only taught her to fight so she could defend herself if she's snatched at again, and even that was too much.

Or maybe how I taught her was too much. I flinch when her screams replay in my brain.

Dad is kind as he speaks to Santos. "Son, do you want me to call one of our healers for her? You boys have been on the road for a long time. I'm sure you could use a break."

"No, Father José. I am her healer. She will be alright if I'm here. It's only when I step away that she gets hurt."

Dad glances at her fresh bandages with a wince. "Oo. The Kalku really did a number on you."

Rafi moves past me and purposefully knocks my body with his shoulder. It wasn't the Kalku who tore her stitches twice. It was me. *I* did a number on her—this woman who'd just been traumatized and taken from her home forever.

It's never been more clear that I am not ready for a wife. Adelita looks so small and content in Santos' arms; I can't picture her doing that with me. Besides, La Sayona won't leave me alone. Just when I let my guard down, she torments me. Bad enough Adelita was subjected to my screams when La Sayona tortured my mind while we were in the motel. It's good she's on Santos' lap. It's good he kisses her braids. It's good he rests his chin atop her head. I don't want anything like that for myself.

Even if I did, it would be impossible anyway.

Why Dad and Eva assumed I was bringing a woman home for myself is beyond me. The fact that they have hope my curse could one day be lifted is sweet, but foolish.

Dad invites Adelita to dinner at his table once she's feeling better. Instead of looking to me when she doesn't know what to do or who to trust, she looks to Santos, who nods. *"You can trust Father José. He's a good man."*

When she can't read his fingers or lips clearly enough, Rafi translates for her. She can't even understand Santos half the time, since his curse left him mute, and yet they appreciate each other so well.

Dad doesn't comment on the fact that it's a definite barrier that Santos can't speak to the woman he adores without a translator present. Instead his eyes soften, looking on the intensity of their connection with wistful eyes, as if it's the best thing he's seen in years. "Santos, I'm so happy you brought her home to us. Good for you, Son. When she's ready, show her around her new home with us, and take her for a walk in the village. Anything she needs, be sure to let the staff know."

"Staff?" she asks.

"Yes, *hija*. Anything at all, my household is at your disposal. Any friend of Santos is… well, usually is only Cruz and Rafael. You are most welcome here."

She snuggles more securely in Santos' arms, and he accommodates her movements.

Jeez, they're like one body. It's so strange to watch, yet oddly comforting.

"What do you do for a living that you have staff that works in your home? Like, you have a housekeeper?" She glances around the room as if seeing all the trappings for the first time. The gold fixtures, the ornate bed, all of it making it dawn on her that she's not in her old life anymore.

Dad casts me an inquiring look, which I ignore. "You want to know what I do? I would've thought Cruz might say that first thing. I'm Chief José, leader of the Cáceres tribe. Cruz didn't tell you any of this?"

Eva breezes by in a flutter of material. "When is the very first possible minute we can spend some time together? All you know of our tribe so far is traveling with three men who have no concept of the finer things."

A smile quirks the corner of Adelita's lips. "What could be finer than motels and gas station food?"

Eva laughs, and for some reason, I exhale. It couldn't possibly matter if my family gets along with Adelita. I mean, for Santos' sake, sure, it makes things less complicated. But it's not like my life would change all that much if Eva and Adelita clashed.

But when Eva takes Adelita's hand and helps her slowly out of the bed, something about the sight feels right. My family likes her. I'm not sure why that matters or even registers, but it does.

Eva doesn't hold back, which is no real surprise. "What are they dressing you in? Santos, honestly. Did you cut her shirt open and retie it?" She closes her eyes as if the whole thing is painful to look at.

I try not to notice the fact that Addy's not wearing a bra.

She has perfectly round, full breasts that lead to a curved waistline and wider hips.

I wet my lips without meaning to and look away.

"The shirt is fine," Adelita lies.

Eva shakes her head, her nose in the air, which is the precursor to her taking over. "Allow me to apologize for my brothers. They've been living on the road for far too long. Santos, take a break. Take a bath. All of you. I've got it from here."

Rafi smirks at my sister. "Good luck getting Santos to let Adelita out of his sight."

Santos does his best to control his anxiety, but it comes out in the rapid and jerky way he signs to Eva. He's careful not to mouth anything so Adelita doesn't catch on. *Do not let her out of your sight, Sister. Please stay in the house. Adelita is injured, so don't let her use her left arm at all. If she needs anything —the smallest thing— I'm to get it for her. I'll be in the kitchen, getting her meal prepared.*

Eva's nose crinkles. "Aarón is serving dinner at the usual time, in like, an hour. Does she have to eat before then?"

"Regular time is fine. I need to make her food. I know Aarón can be trusted, I just... I can't. If Adelita needs something, I will see to it."

I cannot fathom how head over heels a man has to be to have such anxiety over the littlest thing. I mean, Aarón's a fine cook. He's lived with us since before I was born. Santos has never taken issue eating the house chef's food before. He likes Aarón.

It's all too intense for me, so I step out into the hallway and Rafi follows. "How long are we home this time?"

"Just until Santos is stable enough to leave Adelita, so we can go check out the rustling around the curse tree. That's where Tio Bruno wants us." I run my hand over my face. "Man, Santos is so crazy about her. I don't get it. Now he doesn't trust Aarón to cook for her?" I say it like a joke, but I'm truly asking because the whole thing is ridiculous.

Rafi scowls at me, which I gotta say, I'm not a fan of. "It's not Aarón he doesn't trust; it's you. You're the crux of Santos' whole belief system. If Cruz is a good man, other men can be good. Now that Cruz can't be trusted, other men can't be trusted. You really don't get that?" Rafi leans against the wall across from me and kicks his leg up to rest on it. "Look, I get it. You turn into an asshole when you care. I'm under no grand delusion that Cruz the Conqueror has any clue how to deal with real people. But just because Santos and I accept that about you doesn't mean Adelita should. Aside from the fact that you hurt her shoulder twice, you scared Santos. Do you know how hard it is to traumatize a man who survived the Kalku?" Rafi shakes his head and stares up at the ceiling. "I swear, if you take what's good about Santos and break it, you can go on your next mission alone. Adelita is good for him. Lately, you aren't."

Every now and then, I hate that my best friend isn't intimidated by me. Rafi tells me the truth and doesn't feel obligated to hold back. His words smart because they hit too close to the truth. I don't want them to be true, so I ignore them as best I can.

My jaw tightens. "We can stay for a couple days, but then we should get back on the road. Check out the tree."

He fixes me with a steely gaze. "That doesn't sound like an 'I heard you, Rafi. I'll lay off Adelita.'"

I hold up my hands. "Sure. Whatever. Just be ready in a couple days. Santos can sneak in all the kisses he likes with Adelita until then."

Though, to be fair, I've not seen them actually kiss yet.

Rafi levels his gaze at me. "If you ask me, you care a little too much about who she's kissing, Brother." He uses the wall as leverage and kicks himself off it. "I'm staying with Santos until he's okay. If that takes a month, so be it. If you want me along on your missions, you'll fix what you broke before you want to leave for the next job."

He starts to walk away, which makes me brave enough to spout out a mouthy, "Maybe I'll take one of the other warriors who knows how to fall in line."

Rafael laughs at my threat, which irks me. "Typical Cruz. Snarls in the face of the Kalku, but runs like a scared little boy from a conversation with a woman."

Then the bastard starts singing the song the villagers made up about me when I rescued five women from being sacrificed a few years ago. I hate that song, and he friggin' knows it.

I open my mouth to cuss him out, but my words stick in my throat when the door swings open. Eva's arm is threaded through Adelita's, like they've known each other their whole lives. They're giggling about something, but the laughter dies on their lips when they see me standing in their path.

I hate when people do that. I'm not trying to stop people

from laughing, but that's exactly what happens whenever I show up.

Three days. That's how long I can take it before I get itchy and need to be back on the road again. If Rafi's serious about not coming on the next job if I don't work things out with Adelita and Santos in time, I'm screwed. Only Rafi can push me to do something I really don't want to do.

A smile. That's something people like. I catch Adelita's eye and offer up a grin. She freezes and backs up, like I've just told her it's *me* who wants to eat her heart out of her chest, and not the Kalku.

Eva's face pulls in horror. "What is that face for?"

The corners of my mouth fall into my usual grumping. "It's called a smile. Is that not allowed?"

Eva shudders. "If that's what you call a smile, then Brother, you are sorely out of practice."

They leave me standing in the hallway, regretting all the things I can't undo.

Read *Dangerous Hearts* today!

ABOUT THE AUTHOR

USA Today bestselling author Mary E. Twomey lives in Michigan with her three adorable children. She enjoys reading, writing, vegetarian cooking, and telling her children fantastic stories about wombats.

While she loves writing fantasy, dystopian, and paranormal tales for her readers, Mary also writes romance under the name Tuesday Embers.

Visit her online at www.maryetwomey.com, and sign up for her newsletter, so you never miss a new release.